SCARECROW

A Navy vet thought to be dead approaches a plastic surgeon to be 'remade', planning to take his place as heir to a textile mill. Henry Heath, plant manager of the mill, is plotting to take control of the company's stock shares, but playboy Ford Sheppard discovers the scheme and attempts to blackmail him. Then two murders occur within hours of one another — one victim is Ford, the other an artists' model and Heath's mistress. Who is to blame — and how is the strange disfigured man known as the scarecrow involved?

Books by Eaton K. Goldthwaite
in the Linford Mystery Library:

ONCE YOU STOP, YOU'RE DEAD

EATON K. GOLDTHWAITE

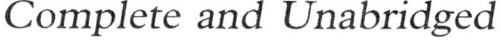

SCARECROW

Complete and Unabridged

LINFORD
Leicester

First published in Great Britain

First Linford Edition
published 2019

*A catalogue record for this book is available
from the British Library.*

ISBN 978–1–4448–4338–5

Published by
F. A. Thorpe (Publishing)
Anstey, Leicestershire

Set by Words & Graphics Ltd.
Anstey, Leicestershire
Printed and bound in Great Britain by
T. J. International Ltd., Padstow, Cornwall

This book is printed on acid-free paper

DEDICATION:

To the Marine Bombing Squadron
433 Southwest Pacific, 1944–1945
whose reports, despite this, have
always gone out on time

1

Painfully he came, stepping down from the high kerb at the intersection above Sudwich Square. His right leg did not function properly, the foot tending to turn inward, and he obviously struggled against it. As he climbed to the sidewalk on the opposite side, you saw that his right shoulder was much too low, and if you looked at his face you were shocked by it.

His face wasn't grotesque or evil or horribly scarred: it had more an unfinished appearance. A thing of clay, abandoned before completion, or perhaps thrust aside to await recurrence of the sculptor's mood.

If you persisted beyond the parody of a face, you saw that this man had strange eyes, coldly blue as the dark waters of the sound eddying about the rocks beyond the village. There was no glimmer of life in those eyes; no sign of recognition of the things about him; yet, as he passed by the bank building and came into the level

1

place by the post office, without so much as glancing down, he raised his twisted foot and extended it to step across a hollowed-out gutter that lay hidden in the path of shadow cast by one of the village's few surviving elms.

Before the entrance walk to the post office, this man stopped and remained without moving — the hesitant act of a lonely man.

People were passing there, on that bright chill morning, but none took particular notice of him. From the post office a tardy clerk appeared, bearing beneath his arm a tri-cone of starred blue. He ran down the steps, slipped through the box hedge, crossed brown-green grass to the pole that had once been a ship's mast. Snapping hooks to eyelets, the clerk ran the cone up fast. And then he was through the hedge again and bounding up the steps.

The unnoticed one stood ludicrously frozen, right arm partially raised, facing the flag.

Henry Heath — portly, bustling manager of the great Kendall-Sudwich mills

— jogged down the steps with arms full of the morning's mail. Mr. Heath, in a hurry, adroitly circled the man without so much as a glance, slipped on a patch of concealed ice, uttered a startled 'Hey!' and dumped the mail through the open window of his Cadillac.

There was a woman in the car and she had not been aware of the man either. Her carefully rouged face had been absorbed in the task of applying a liquid polish to her nails.

As the mail cascaded around her, the woman uttered a scream, and her voice cut the square with the brittleness of breaking glass.

'You clumsy fool! Why don't you look what you're doing?'

And then she was out on the sidewalk, glaring in rage at the spreading stain on topcoat and skirt. Her eyes flashed anger, and she trembled with uncontrolled rage.

'You clumsy *fool*!'

Less than a yard away, the unnoticed man shivered and drew back against the hedge. Mr. Heath, red-faced and bustling, began to gather the scattered mail.

His quick eyes appraised the rigid stranger, noticed now, and jumped beyond to scan the square. His eyes caught and clouded thoughtfully at two distant but approaching figures. And then he bent about the business of gathering the last of the letters.

'Sorry. I slipped,' Heath said gruffly.

'You're *sorry*? Look at this damned dress. Ruined! This stuff will never come out — and on my *new* spring coat. Look at it!'

Mr. Heath sat himself firmly behind the wheel. 'Come along,' he said.

'I will not! Who are you to order me around after ruining my clothes?'

'Please! We're not alone.'

Mr. Heath's brusque manner had fled; for an incredibly stout woman, flanked by an equally stout woman, alike as stone and pebble, were nearing with undulating progress.

Their heads bobbed and turned in unison; their bright eyes missed not a single detail; their voices parroted to the echo, 'Good morning, Mr. Heath — Good morning, Mr. Heath . . . '

4

Mr. Heath miserably wished them a good morning and waited for them to enter the post office. Then, in swift and direct pleading he said: 'Tessie, for heaven's sake, please! You know I'll buy you new clothes. Only stop making a scene.'

For the first time, it seemed, the woman became aware of the stiff and shivering figure by the hedge. She turned to survey him insolently, and then her eyebrows drew together and a puzzled light entered her eyes. For a moment she stood, staring at the stranger, who stopped his trembling and became as immutable and unfathomable as stone.

'Tessie! Please! We're very late.'

Shrugging, the woman swept her glance from the stranger and pegged haughtily around; the car door slammed and the whine of hastening tyres faded beyond the square.

In the corner of his retreat, the stranger stood hesitant against the bitter wind. His eyes were cast down, fixed upon the sliver of Mr. Heath's embarrassing ice. Or perhaps on the vivid spatter of nail polish gleaming where the woman's hand had angrily flung it, blood-like, in the sun.

A postman, weighted by the heavy saddle of his mail sack, came around the angle of red brick wall to pass through an opening in the box hedge. Although not young, he held himself very erect. His glasses had slid down his nose and he was trying to get them back in place by wriggling his nose, rabbit fashion.

The postman stiffened as he saw the sagging, apathetic man. Through the round panes that grotesquely enlarged them, the postman's eyes began at the faded and shapeless green hat resting low over pointed ears, searched downward with swift minuteness; saw and puzzled over the too-low shoulder, the gaunt frame, the tired, turned-in foot.

And then, readjusting his burden, he came on down the walk. Pausing, he smiled encouragement and said:

'Kind of brisk this morning. Going to be warm after a while, though.'

The gaunt man looked at the postman out of eyes that were nearly black and expressionless. There seemed to be in him the urge to reply, for the muscles about

6

his slash of a mouth moved twitchingly, as if he had forgotten how to speak.

And then the opportunity was lost, for in that moment a small car drew up to the kerb to discharge a broad, muscular and completely excited man.

'We've been looking all over for you,' the excited man said in a strained voice. 'Don't ever do that again!'

Into the gaunt man's eyes a swift, faint light came, only to die as swiftly. Shrugging, he allowed himself to be led, entered the car and was whisked away.

'Well!'

Puzzled, the postman stared, and then resumed his march, bracing himself against the bitter wind. He scowled fiercely. It had all happened pretty quickly, but he'd noticed that it was a woman who was driving the car. And he thought he knew who the woman was.

But the old relic who had been standing there, him with his clothing hung scarecrow-like on his skinny body, a stick against the cold March wind. Just why had he given the decrepit antique a second glance? Had he thought that the battered reed reminded him of someone? And if so, who could it possibly be?

'Durned mysterious,' the postman said under his breath. 'I'll swear that was old man Kendall's car, and it was his daughter-in-law that was drivin' it. But the scarecrow, and the excited fellow that looked like a wrestler, I never set eyes on before in my life. Now what would she be doin' with them?'

★　★　★

Frederick Thorne limped away from his easel, stood with his back to it for a moment, and then slowly turned. He had a dramatic way of standing and turning; although the withering finger of paralysis had touched his leg, there was distinction in him. In his narrow, ascetic face and the severe pompadour of his straight yellow hair, in his unbending aloofness, was the mark of the man who, by choice, walks alone.

Transferring a bundle of brushes from his right hand to his left, he ran paint-stained fingers through his yellow hair and critically examined his work.

'It's coming along,' his voice boomed. 'That'll be all for today, Morgan. I'll need you again tomorrow. Same time as today, if you can make it.'

Tessie Morgan stirred, pushed herself up from the couch and stretched. It had not been a difficult pose; none of Frederick Thorne's ever were. But there was something about Mr. Thorne that turned the simplest things into lots of work. There was a certain magnetism about him that demanded, and received, a great deal of response even while you were lying perfectly still, and you had to lie still if you didn't want to be sworn at.

Posing for Frederick Thorne was just like acting in a play without the benefit of being permitted to move around or speak any lines.

The woman quickly tired of pretending to be tired and, posing prettily against braced arms, watched Thorne as he frowned at his canvas. Her eyes followed him as he moved to deposit his brushes in a cracked pitcher on a stand next the easel. She idly wondered if he might be as rich as he was famous, and whether or not she would like being married to him. She knew she would like the clothes he could buy her, and she would enjoy sharing the homage that was his wherever he went.

Her full lips tightened and her eyes grew dark. 'He won't look at me, damn him,' she thought. 'All the time he's painting me he isn't really looking at me. All I am to him is just so many bumps and curves.'

Her eyes sultry, the woman searched with her toes until she located furred moccasins, slid them on and stepped down from the stand. Avoiding the artist, who was cleaning his brushes, she stalked beyond him, shamelessly naked and disdainful haughty, and stood to examine what he had wrought.

The painting was of large size, an 'exhibition piece' he had termed it. She was but one of a half-dozen figures there; beneath an arbour men and women sat about a table, drinking red wine. In the painting it appeared that she had had too much, for she lay sprawled on a leafy bed. Most of the figures were laughing at her, but one was not; his face was angry and he was attempting to cover her nakedness with a shawl.

She decided that the painting did not do her justice. The pose didn't suit her, and she didn't like being laughed at, not even in a picture. She supposed that this was 'art', but she hoped that someday Mr. Thorne would paint her as she really wanted to be painted, posed before a mirror in filmy black lingerie.

She turned challengingly. 'I can come tomorrow, if you want me to.'

'Eh? Oh, good. At what time?'

'Any time. In the morning if you want me to.'

'But what about your job at the mill as Heath's secretary?'

The woman scowled.

'Heath! Ugh! That clumsy fool. You know what he did? He spilled a full bottle of nail polish all over my *new* coat and dress. This morning, right in front of the post office. In front of a lot of people!'

Thorne was slopping turpentine on his hands. A sudden grin gave an impish cast to his features.

'Nail polish? Didn't know that Heath used the stuff.'

'Silly! *He* wasn't using it, *I* was! He practically threw the whole morning mail at me while I was sitting in the car. Tried to tell me he slipped! Believe me, I told *him*!'

'I believe you.'

The woman smiled suddenly, baring beautifully strong translucent teeth.

'Anyway, he promised me he'd buy me a new coat and dress.'

The painter dried his hands on a grimy towel and reached for a worn blue corduroy jacket.

'It won't be necessary for you to work for me in the morning,' he said. 'Myself, I like to sleep late. And besides, there must be some time when you're supposed to show up at the mill. I wouldn't want to be the cause of your losing a job.'

The woman gave a throaty laugh.

'Lose my job? That's pretty good! And who would fire me — Mister Henry Heath, perhaps? Ho, ho! Maybe you didn't know it was the old man *himself* who gave me my job!'

Her head came down, bringing brightly amused eyes to bear on this Thorne, and her fine dark hair, freed by the movement, fell to brush her shoulders.

He stiffened. 'Get into your clothes and get out of here,' he said quietly.

She did not move.

'Mr. Heath doesn't know I'm posing for you, naked . . . ' She lingered over the word. 'And Ben Sutts doesn't know, either. If Ben knew, he'd be sore. I wouldn't like to see what Ben would do if he found out.'

'Oh, Judas Priest! Will you get into your clothes and go home?'

The woman laughed again, and started for the lacquered screen that hid the dressing alcove.

'Ben'll know,' she threw back over her shoulder, 'when he sees the picture. He always goes to the Sudwich gallery every year.' She stopped and turned, swiftly anxious. 'You're going to show it in the Sudwich gallery, aren't you?'

Thorne exploded in wrath.

'Ben Sutts! That fishmonger! Who gives a potted ham what Ben Sutts thinks? Or

13

what Fatty Heath thinks, or for that matter, what Sudwich thinks? Do you think I paint for them? Heath! I'd love to have a view of his face when he folds his hands across his belly and stares at a nude. I can see him now, licking his lips and then turning around to his mousy wife to say, 'Prue, the thing's indecent!' Heath! Sutts! What sort of people are they? Do you think that anyone in Sudwich, with the single exception of Ford Sheppard, cares enough about art to pay thirty-five hundred dollars for a painting? Your friend Sutts wouldn't pay that much for the gallery. *Will you get dressed?*'

The last was directed, in a roar, to the woman.

She had appeared, in chemise, ready to defend her Ben Sutts if not Henry Heath and Sudwich. But Frederick Thorne's savage mien discouraged argument. In place of defence, she compromised by making a face. And thereafter her accumulation of clothing was swift, ending at the door when she viciously jammed on her hat.

'Just see if I come back tomorrow! Just see if I come back here at all!'

'I don't give a damn what you do. D'you think you're the only woman in Connecticut who's got a body?'

'Ben Sutts is not a fishmonger! He's a contract fisherman. He owns the *Tessie M* — in case you'd like to know, it's named after *me*! And he's an important man; he's being put up for selectman this year. Oh, you — you make me so damn *mad*!'

And thereupon she departed, her exit being only a little marred by the automatic closing device which prevented the heavy door from slamming.

Thorne scowled after her. Damned wildcat, he thought. *Probably shouldn't've laid it on quite so thick; would be devilish embarrassing if she walked out on me at this point. Maybe I should have gotten someone else to pose for this one; someone like Marion Kendall. Kendall's got a beautiful figure — Diana, the huntress. And wouldn't that raise a stink in Sudwich. Bet she would've jumped at the chance; she must be lonely as hell. But no. This one is for Morgan. The full-blown, lush and peasant. She'll be back. She won't quit as long as she thinks there's a chance of displaying her navel in the Sudwich gallery.*

He turned, surveying his work again, and presently began to hum. It was beginning to jell, and it would be a good one. Like all his work, this one would draw them. They would look at the others, making little notes in the margins of their programmes. They would examine each one with swift, professional mercilessness, saving his until the last. And then they would scan his work, inch-square by inch-square; to guess at his palette and marvel at his technique. The work of Fred Thorne was good enough to endure.

Suddenly tired, he stepped back, dragging his leg, and limping to the door opened it and stepped out for a view of his realm.

The hush of dusk was on the chill air, bearing the promise of yet another freezing night before winter's stiff back would finally be broken. Before him,

16

reed-grown dunes extended to the dark restless waters of the sound, and to his left the Dunes Road stretched away, curving about the inner bay to the distant blaze of light that was the great Kendall-Sudwich mill.

Distant and diminishing on the road, a coupé's red rear light winked. That would be the outraged Tessie, homeward bound. A sardonic grin lighted Thorne's face. A good thing he hadn't told Tessie the painting was for the Carnegie and not for Sudwich; if he'd told her that, she would have quit him for sure.

Night was growing swiftly. Out on the water an intermittent message of warning from the light on William's Reef was guiding a brave little fleet of three lobster-boats that were headed for the narrow mouth of the Sudwich channel.

Thorne stood stiff against the unrelenting wind, and his mind sped swiftly backward to the night in which he had first stood in these dunes, watching the light on William's Reef and the lobster-boats coming in. There hadn't been a warm studio at his back then; there hadn't been much of anything except a broken marriage and a smashed business career and a desire to be alone. There hadn't even been a desire to paint, not then. But he had found something in the dark brooding waters and the inquisitive light and the brave little boats; something solid and enduring and deeply satisfying; something that had not changed despite the awesome changes of the world all around it.

A long way out on the sound, the blot that was Sixpence Island suddenly raised a searching light-finger skyward. Thorne stiffened and glared at the moving pencil of light. And then abruptly surrendering, he withdrew to the warmth of his studio.

Shivering, hands thrust deep in the pockets of his jacket, he started his dragging way towards the kitchen only to stop at a point just past the screened alcove. On the wall nearest him was a framed pastel head of a youth. A moody face, turned halfway away, so that you saw the taut line of the jaw, the small rounded ear, the finely shaped head under its cap of dark, curling hair, the whole alive, immortalized by Thorne's own unerring touch.

His eyes clouded for a moment, and in the dark pool of memory he saw a lad sailing a rakish red snipe, bringing tobacco and food and companionship to an unknown artist. Companionship? It was more wide-eyed worship. A shy lad, gravely contemplating the threat of Thorne's knight and the jeopardy of his own queen. A lad quietly munching one of Thorne's heathenish sandwiches while he listened to the flood of ideas that came leaping, full-formed, from a changing concept of life.

A lonely lad, at first, whose mother had just died. And then with the alchemy of nature, filling out and shooting up, changing to a man who was simple and direct and unaffected by the wealth of his father.

'Cotton Kendall,' Thorne sighed. 'Cotton, you poor swine. Why must I always think of you when I see that cursed light?'

★   ★   ★

Tessie Morgan did not immediately go home. Not that she could have gone

19

'home' had she so desired; in her own characteristic and definitely final way, she had slammed the door of that sanctuary all too completely.

With her rising affluence as secretary, first to old man Kendall and later to Mr. Heath, and as occasional model to the great Mr. Thorne, Tessie had decided she could afford an establishment of her own. And thereupon she had crashed headlong into a will as stubborn and a temper as violent as her own. There had been words which were nasty, even for Mill Street. United for once, Pa and Ma Morgan had collaborated on an opinion which amounted to an unlovely prediction. Tessie's retort had been some unsavoury family history, no slight castigation of her own origin.

There had been a climax in the form of a physical display, and the dove of peace, timidly borne in the hands of neighbours, took flight before Ma Morgan's accurately pitched crockery.

And so Tessie took an apartment, a two-room-and-bath affair above Kessler's grocery store. It was the sole living quarters in the building, the rest being devoted to housing the surplus stock of the rugged individualist who held forth downstairs. Tessie did not mind the absence of immediate neighbours. She had a telephone, which was more than the Mill Street Morgans had, and if she wanted company she was not long in finding it.

She'd had a grand time fixing up the place. Everything, from the canopied bed to the red-enamelled hall door was her own idea. And there was a nice room for her precious dining-room furniture.

Mr. Heath had looked it all over carefully, no doubt with an approving eye on the entrance to the alley which led both to Dock Street and to the rear of the unoccupied filling station on Liberty Street. Mr. Heath had put his arm around her and called her 'a brave woman who deserved a break,' and had offered to help.

Tessie scowled in memory of Mr. Heath and pointed the nose of her coupé up the Dunes Road. The coupé, a Ford, had been financed with the assistance of Ben Sutts. While it was to be admitted

21

that the assistance thus far had consisted of the down payment and all of the instalments, she intended to take it up just as soon as she got the rug and her portable typewriter paid for.

It didn't pay for a woman to be too much in debt to a fellow like Ben Sutts.

It was on his account that she had no intention of going straight to the apartment. At seven o'clock Tessie had a date with Sutts to go to the movies. Well, after the fight she'd just had with Mr. Thorne, sitting through a stuffy movie and being pawed at by Ben Sutts would be *impossible*. Let the big lug stew in his own juice. Just who did he think he was, and what made him so damned confident that she'd marry him when he got ready to ask her?

Of course, he did *seem* to care for her. Anyway, he was jealous. He had proved that by adding a generous splatter of crimson to the red-enamelled front door. The crimson had come from the aristocratic nose of Ford Sheppard, and Ford Sheppard was the only man in Sudwich who would pay thirty-five hundred dollars for a painting.

Thirty-five hundred dollars!

There had been a possibility that Ford Sheppard might have helped to pay for the furniture, and it had been his first — well, almost his first — visit when the awful thing had happened. And he hadn't been doing anything wrong. He'd just been calling for her to take her out, to drive in his Packard all the way to New Haven to a night club.

That had been six months ago, and Ford Sheppard hadn't been back.

If only Bill hadn't joined the Marines and gone off to fight the Japanese. Maybe Bill was a mill boy and poor, but he was the best-looking fellow in Sudwich, with the possible exception of Cotton Kendall; Bill was the football star of Sudwich High. And she had been Bill's woman. They were going to be married; hadn't he told her, before he went away, that if she ever so much as *looked* at another man he'd come back and kill her?

Funny, this was the second time today she'd thought of Bill. The first had been in the morning, when she saw that horrible-looking man in front of the post office, right after Mr. Heath had ruined her dress. Why should she have thought of Bill then?

Poor Bill! Both he and Cotton Kendall, missing in action for almost five months now. And Bill's family, although she and they weren't on the best of terms, hadn't had a single word since.

There was one comfort, though. Mutual grief had made her a new friend. Cotton Kendall's wife had been wonderful. So brave and sweet and understanding. And what *she* was going through, with that sick old man on her hands . . .

Tessie scowled at her reflection in the unclean windshield.

'Damn it,' she said aloud. 'I wonder why it is I want Mr. Thorne to *kiss* me?'

★ ★ ★

At half-past eight Thorne had completed his customary walk through the dunes and should have been ready to settle down to an hour's reading of *The New York Times*. The newspaper had been poked through the slot in his door at eight that

24

morning and, as always, there it had remained.

But this night Thorne did not rescue his *Times* and sit in his accustomed chair by the fireplace. Instead, he paced in aimless circles, and finally, against his will, to the window on the sound side where, drawing the curtain, he glared in frustrated wrath at the pencils of light, three now, above Sixpence Island.

'That's it,' he said bitterly. 'That's how they did it. They caught you in the crossbeams, and you never had a chance.'

Dropping the curtain with angry gesture, he dragged his leg to a carved teakwood box that stood in solitary grandeur on the only un-littered table in the room. His fingers, ugly in contrast to their great gift, lingered absently, caressing the artistry of the box, but his mind was already inside and brooding over the contents. Letters, twenty of them; one for each month that Cotton Kendall had been away. Graphic letters that told of a new world.

He opened the box, and taking the bottom letter from it, limped to his fireside chair. And as he crossed his studio, he switched off the overhead fluorescent light. Only the lamp, precariously perched on the rough stone hearth, remained to bathe him and the worn letter in his hands in a huddled, lonely glow.

The much-read letter was captioned 'VMSB-306, care of Fleet Post Office, San Francisco,' carried the simple legend 'Southwest Pacific,' and was dated the twenty-sixth of October.

'*Dear Maestro,*' it began. '*We are now nicely settled in our new location, and I am glad to report that it is completely free of mosquitoes. There are practically no cases of malaria on the island, a welcome contrast from the last place; we are living in screened huts, quite comfortably, and except for the usual dehydrated vegetables, the food is most satisfactory. There is an excellent beach not a hundred yards from my hut, and I make frequent use of it.*

'*We are getting along all right, and thus far have been very lucky.*

'*Maestro, I have a request to make . . .*'

★   ★   ★

He shivered suddenly in the presence of a draught, real or fancied, that touched him with icy fingers. Though severe, the chill passed quickly, dispelled by the warmth of the fire beside him, and he resumed his reading.

⋆ ⋆ ⋆

' . . . a request that, coming from me, may seem a bit strange. Mind, I am not afraid. I am as confident that I will return home as I was once certain that your paintings would hang in the Metropolitan. But I am also sensible. I realize that this is a grim business, and we are playing for keeps. So that if anything should happen to me, I want you to urge Marion to leave Sudwich; to go somewhere new and start again. You see, I love her enough that I can't bear to think of her being buried with dad in that huge old house, attempting to keep up the tradition of being Cotton Kendall's widow.

'Do that for me, Maestro. Just that. I realize that you may not have hit it off too *well, but I know she will listen to you. And she is my wife . . . '*

★ ★ ★

Frederick Thorne closed his eyes. A strange, strong-willed yet sentimental man, this worker who had been touched by greatness. He could banish disagreeable thoughts from his mind with the facility of closing a drawer, but the last half of Cotton Kendall's letter would forever remain to shake him each time a sword of light stabbed the dark sky:

★ ★ ★

'I guess that in every letter I've written of Bill Stanczyk, my gunner since we've been overseas. He was born in Sudwich and he worked in the mill, but I had to come halfway across the world to find him. The other night while we were over target, a strange thing happened to us. We had come in on our first run, and the flak was very thick. The lights boxed us nicely, and we bounced a lot, but that

28

was all. We left our calling cards, and then, when we came back on our second run, it happened.

'Of course the lights nailed us at once. They're operated by sound-detecting device, and a single-engined plane hasn't a chance to dodge them. It was an eerie feeling, suspended in that bath of light, but what made it strangest of all was that there was no flak.

'I couldn't figure it out, but Bill could. 'Get going!' his yell came over the interphone. 'They've got a bogey up above us!'

'Neat, wasn't it? The Japs knew we'd be watching and cursing the lights below, and wouldn't be apt to look up; they'd stopped throwing flak because they didn't want to hit their own plane . . . '

* * *

'Maestro!

Frederick Thorne opened his eyes and stared incredulously into the shadow beyond his circle of light.

'Maestro, do you hear me?'

The voice was hoarse, low and unrecognizable. It seemed to come from the darkness behind the lacquered screen hiding the alcove. No, not *seemed*. This voice was real, corporeal, earthly.

Frederick Thorne stiffened and started to rise.

'Who are you, and what do you want?' he heard himself ask.

There was movement behind the screen; a shuffling change of position, a deep sigh.

'Don't get up, and do not be alarmed. I have been here for some time, thinking of what I would say to you. I had not realized just how hard it would be.'

'Look here,' Thorne said hoarsely. 'If it's money you want, or this is some kind of trick, you can save your breath!'

'There is no trick, and I do not want money. I ask only that you hear what I have to say. You must hear me through so that when I am finished, there will be no doubt in your mind as to who I am. No matter if, should you chance to see me, you do not see in me the semblance of anyone you have ever known. You must

30

recognize me, not from the way I sound or appear, but from what I will reveal myself to be.'

'I'm not interested in your game,' Thorne bridled. 'Unless you leave at once, I shall call the police.'

'Yes? Think! Remember back — it was Nineteen Thirty or Thirty-one. You had spent a week at the Appletons' and then you came down to these dunes and rented old Lazear's fishing-shack. It was in June, early June, and you were on the beach painting those two rocks down near the spot where Ford Sheppard later built Robber's Roost. You were painting, and a boy came along in a red snipe, beached her, and came up to watch you. You were nasty to him at first, and he said, '*Sir, I meant no harm.*''

Beads of perspiration gathered on Thorne's forehead. Gripping the arms of his chair, he leaned forward and an agonized cry wrenched from his throat.

'Good God! It isn't possible!'

'No? Don't be too sure. And don't get up. I'm armed, and I warn you that I'll shoot you down if you try to look at me

31

. . . This boy came back, day after day. Sometimes he brought food; Rhode Island johnny-cake meal and McIntosh apples and Canadian bacon. Sometimes he brought tobacco; 'Old Sailor's Delight' was the name of it . . . '

The voice died away.

Frederick Thorne sat very still, suddenly relaxed, conscious of the sweat that was coursing down his cheeks.

'I believe I understand,' he said slowly. 'I have read of these things and have heard of them happening to people, but I never took any stock in them. I sat here thinking of you, seeing you very clearly, picturing you exactly as you were, suspended in those horrible lights. And so it has happened to me, to a man who doesn't believe in God or in much of anything.'

'It isn't quite like that, Maestro.' The voice was becoming very tired. 'You have an idea that I'm dead and this is some sort of miracle of reincarnation, and I can't say that I blame you. But it isn't quite that way. Perhaps one day I may tell you the story of the past months, but not now. I can only tell you now that I am not dead. But I can't permit you to look at me, not yet. And, if this wild hope of mine should fade, maybe never. But you've got to help me. You're the only one who can.'

Frederick Thorne clasped his great ugly hands together and began, gently, to rock back and forth on the hearth. Unashamed tears streaked down his face as he whispered:

'Cotton, you poor swine. What have they done to you?'

2

It was a strange request that the voice made. In his chair, the painter sat with fingertips pressed together and eyes thoughtfully avoiding the lacquered screen. Gone now was his initial shock; there remained only an infinite sadness.

'I think I understand,' he said slowly. 'All your hopes are contingent upon the work of the surgeon. Should he be successful, as you hope, then you could resume your normal life. Is that it?'

'Yes.'

'And if he should not be successful?'

'I — I'd rather not think of that just now. I'll meet it when — if it comes.'

Thorne shook his head slowly.

'Naturally, you are assuming no change here in Sudwich. You are taking for granted that only you yourself have changed. Do you believe that in this lapse of two years your wife, Marion, and your father have gone on being just as they were when last you knew them?'

'Is there any reason for me to believe otherwise?'

'Possibly. I don't know.' Thorne's eyes filmed and his voice took on a trace of huskiness. 'Cotton, I'm not trying to argue with you. God alone knows what you must have suffered and are suffering now. But I can't permit you to build your hopes only to have them destroyed. I am thinking of you, the real you that is Cotton Kendall, not the mould that you are contained in.'

'Nothing more could happen to me. If I succeed, I shall be grateful; if not, nothing more. You'll let me have the pastel, then?'

'It is yours. And this thing you are planning will cost money. Let me help you, in the form of a loan if you insist. I can let you have a couple of thousand tomorrow night, or more if you need it.'

'I — I — thank you. I have enough.'

'And you are all right in the meantime? You have a comfortable place to stay?'

'I am all right.'

'You could sleep here, in my extra room, I won't disturb you, or attempt to spy on you.'

'I'd rather not. Turn out the light now. I shall be going.'

Thorne's hand hesitated. 'You'll return, then, tomorrow night?'

'I'd rather not say. It isn't that I don't trust you. God knows, if I hadn't trusted you more than anyone else I would never have come here. But I've got so much to straighten out — so much to do. Turn out the light, Maestro.'

Thorne lingered in desperation. 'I can't let you go like this, sick and alone.'

'I'm not sick, Maestro. The light. Now!'

Thorne's reluctant hand closed on the hot brass cylinder; his fingers pressed the switch, and blanketing darkness rushed from the studio's corners.

There was a shuffling noise behind the lacquered screen; a quick intake of breath as if in repression of pain; a tiny scratching sound. Thorne, straining, saw only the vaguest of dark shapes filter past the screen's edge and through the kitchen door. For a wild instant he fought against a desire to press the switch, still hot under his hand. And then he heard the creak of a board and felt the swift shock of cold air.

Thorne started up from his chair and called out, a hoarse, inarticulate cry. His hand groped to the lamp switch and brought the glowing circle of light into being.

When he could see, he saw that his studio was as it had been — except that the pastel head was gone.

★　★　★

At ten minutes before ten, a Packard coupé rolled noiselessly down Sudwich's Mizzen Hill Road, turned right at the bottom to enter Liberty Street, and passing Baumgard's deserted filling station came to rest in the deep pool of darkness between Johnson's feed store and the high ledge upon which Mizzen Hill was built.

The Packard's sole occupant, Ford Sheppard, glanced at himself in the faintly reflected glow of the rear-vision mirror and ran an approving hand along his grey-templed head. Giving a final touch to his tie, he leaned back against the wide leather seat and began to hum in concert with his softly playing radio.

He frowned at the luminous dial of the dashboard clock. In just a few minutes now, the door on the kerb side would open and *she* would be there. She would be wearing a fox jacket and with her would be the faint, exciting odour of gardenia. She would be hatless, and her burnished auburn hair would be piled in a mass of tight ringlets above her ears.

She would stand a moment, smiling, and in her huskily low yet incisively clear voice would say, 'Hello, I'm in luck! Going my way?'

And then, without nervousness or silly modesty, without glancing back or around, she would get in beside him. She would gather her skirt while he leaned past her to close the door. And while he was closing the door, she would whisper 'Darling,' and her warm and mysterious lips would brush his ear.

Ford Sheppard moistened his lips, and his hand strayed to the glove compartment where a bottle of Scotch whisky waited. His hand stopped.

'No, got to watch it,' he said to his

image in the dark windshield. 'Not so young as I used to be. Got to make up my mind. Do I want to go on having a good time and someday go *pop*, or do I want to slow down and grow old?'

He wondered what it would be like to be really old, and then he thought of her and his body grew warm.

Wonder how this one's lasted so long? Can't be love. Love's for nincompoops who are always mooning and getting themselves pregnant; stuffy people who have jobs and eat breakfast and raise lots of kids. Love's a thing the willing party keep reminding the unwilling party to keep reminding them of. Something they keep saying over and over so much they get to believe it.

Sheppard frowned and wondered just how it had begun. Of course, she'd always been there; the gawky kid next door, always climbing the fence and mooning around. And then, presto! Blossoming into a beauty. But that year he'd been interested in — who was it? Somebody. This one had been there a long time, years, before he'd done anything about it.

Must have finally started while they were dancing together. Two or three months ago at somebody's party. That was when such things usually started. You sensed a response and you held her a little tighter. Maybe you breathed in her ear, or just brushed her hair with your lips. Then you saw that look come into her eyes, and you felt a thrill of exultation all the way down to your heels.

If she was married, that was where the gentleman bowed out and did some damned silly thing like going on a long cruise or plunging into business or joining a crusade. Or getting good and soused.

Funny, this one hadn't cost a penny. She wouldn't even let him buy her flowers. She was smart. Flowers would start all kinds of a row. The old man would be suspicious about flowers. The old man knew everything that happened in his mausoleum of a house, sick as he was, even to the birth of mice in the kitchen walls. The old man knew even more about what went on in the mill than did his son-in-law, Henry Heath, whom he was paying to be its manager. Did the old man know about

Heath and the Morgan wench? Probably. Probably the old man even knew about *them*.

Not that it made a damned bit of difference.

Sheppard wondered if women ever bought flowers for themselves. His mother had bought herself all manner of potted petunias, begonias, geraniums and the like. At one time the Sheppard manse had resembled a botanical garden. That was in the good old days, when *pere* Sheppard was trying, successfully, to corner half the traction companies in New England.

'She's late tonight,' he said.

He wished she'd let him take her to New York, to show her off. Of course, under the circumstances, they couldn't. *I wonder*, he mused soberly, *if I could be in love?*

Ford Sheppard in love? How long would it last if they had to get up in the morning together and have their hangovers together? Night after night, to go home and take mutual parts in the process of deglamorization; to wake up and watch the lump of bed clothing that was your wife — gosh!

Suddenly, he felt an acute distaste for himself.

I'm rotten. A pure hedonist. Never done a damned constructive thing in my life. I've been the kind of a guy that, if I was the right kind of a guy, I'd punch in the mouth. Why couldn't I have let her alone? She's different, really a wonderful person. She's not like the others. I wonder if, when all this business is cleared away, she would marry me?

He straightened with a guilty start, his reverie interrupted by a rustle of movement. On the kerb side, a darker form materialized in the darkness; the door handle turned downward and the shock of cold air swept in.

She stood a moment, nestling her chin in the tightly held collar of her fox jacket, and regarded him seriously. 'Hello! I'm in luck,' she said in her throaty, softly musical voice. 'Going my way?'

It was funny, how many times she could say it and each time give it a different sound.

★ ★ ★

For a long time, Thorne sat in his chair by the open hearth. His first fragmentary and disordered thoughts had prompted him to run after Cotton Kendall and capture him and, if necessary, force him to return to the warmth and protection of the studio. And then the voice of reason had bade him remain.

Even a friendship such as theirs bore no privilege of violation of the rights of privacy. Cotton had had his reasons for not wanting to reveal himself. Probably he was horribly disfigured. And, while he might not realize it, he was also mentally ill. He was afraid of the consequences to himself of a meeting without the protection of an obscuring screen. A forced meeting could bring him irreparable harm.

It was deep-rooted, this fear of his, and he was staking his hopes on the hand of an unnamed plastic surgeon to pluck it out. Frederick Thorne had been in that other war, and he knew how great the problem of readjustment had been

without the added obstacle of disfigure-
ment. And Thorne remembered Paris,
where he had spent a year belatedly
studying the art he was beginning to
grasp so well.

Paris, the city where fifteen years after
that first great war, the unfortunate living
were allowed to walk a restricted area
only at night because the people must not
see.

He shuddered. No, Cotton Kendall
could not be helped in that way.

He arose, and with his slow, dragging
step went to his front door and opened it.
Beyond the brick path with its straggling
hedge, the lonely dunes lay dark and cold,
an exhausted sterile giant wasted by the
unequal struggle against the voracious
sound. Scudding clouds obscured the
slender moon, and for the moment his
enemies, the searchlights, were sleeping
and Sixpence Island was no more
distinguishable than the waters about it.
Only William's Reef Light, faithful friend,
kept up its vigil.

He sighed, and a great heaviness lay in
his heart for the one out there who had

crossed those dunes, bearing a pastel portrait under his arm as if it were Aladdin's lamp. What surgeon in the world was there that could mould a head to conform to a picture? What mortal lived who could restore youth's bright colours and brave smile? And what would happen to the hopeful one when the last bandage was unwrapped and he came to face a mirror?

'I should not have let him go,' Thorne said.

And then he was brought from his reverie by the distant approach of headlights on the Dunes road. Fast nearing, they grew in intensity as they followed the sweeping curve of the bay. If that car held someone who was coming to visit him . . .

Swiftly he drew back into his studio and glanced at his watch. A quarter past ten. Not too late for some fool to come soliciting, or just hoping to mooch a nightcap.

Extinguishing the lights, he waited and watched the road through the square of glass in his door. One minute; two; three. The car did not slow; its lights flashed past and its noise diminished.

He was conscious of relief. That had probably been Ford Sheppard, on his drunken way to Robber's Roost. Flicking on the lights, he moved to his telephone, hesitant no longer. Regardless of what he should or should not have done while Cotton Kendall was in the studio, there was one thing he could do now. Finding the number he sought, he called it, and after an interminable ringing a sleepy voice answered.

Thorne said, 'I want to speak to Mr. Kendall on a matter of the utmost importance.'

'Mr. Kendall? Why, that's impossible! He's a very sick man, and has left strict orders not to be disturbed.'

'I realize all that. Do you think I'd call him about trifles at this hour? I must speak to him!'

'But you can't, I tell you! Mr. Kendall is terrible sick. The doctor was here tonight and told me himself that Mr. Kendall — Say, who is this calling?'

Thorne said grimly: 'Never mind. I'm coming to the house, and you can tell him

I'll be there in fifteen minutes. Don't argue. *Tell him!'*

★　★　★

Ford Sheppard stopped the Packard on a tiny stretch of beach between two great rocks. Ahead of them, a powerful ray burst upon the dark sky and poked an inquisitive finger at the scurrying clouds. Far back and to their left, a solitary dim square located Thorne's lone studio, and on the rustling water that reached before them an intermittent dancing path gave a reminder of William's Light, hidden from direct view by the great sheltering rock.

'Y'know,' Sheppard said, 'I feel strange. As if I'd grown up all of a sudden. I think it's time we talked seriously about us. This far it's been wonderful, but even a damned fool like me knows that it can't go on forever. Someday we'll be caught or seen or some Sudwich snoop will guess, and then there'll be hell to pay.'

She turned from looking at the water. 'Is someone talking?' she asked.

'No, not that I know of. We've been

damned careful. Too careful to suit me. Haven't seen as much of you as I'd like, not by half. But I suppose that's the price one has to pay.'

Her eyes regarded him speculatively. 'You're quite sure you've heard nothing?'

'Absolutely, Marion. I have friends, y'know, and they're the type who at first breath would come to me and say, 'Look here, Shep, old man. I hate to butt into a man's private affairs, but there's something I think you ought to know.' Oh, we're in the clear, all right.'

'Then why are you worrying?'

'Been wondering, that's all. Just what do you think of me? You must think there's nothing in my head but pleasure — fun and smart remarks and drinking and having a good time throwing away the patrimony. God knows I've never given anyone reason to think otherwise.'

'Haven't I come just as far along this road as you have?' she asked.

He gave her a sideways glance. 'You have, sweet. And from your standpoint you've come a lot farther than I have. That's why I'm damned if I can figure it out. Frankly you're much too nice a woman to be having an affair with a rotter like me.'

'Oh, so it's an affair, is it?' She smiled. 'Well, let's put it down to your irresistible charm. After all, I'm only a woman, you know.'

'And a very lovely one. Look, I don't seem to be making such a good job of this. What I'm trying to get out is that maybe I seem to be all froth, but there's more to me than that, and I want you to know it.'

She smiled pensively, and her fingers touched his arm. 'I like you as you are. There are some things one doesn't have to say. Under the circumstances, perhaps it would be better if they were left unsaid.'

'That's just it. Look, Marion. I'm forty. But I don't feel any different now than I did when I was your age. I can still take on anyone in the club at tennis, and I haven't shot higher than a seventy-six since I can remember. But damn it, that isn't getting me anywhere, and what good is anything if it doesn't get you somewhere?'

'Oh! So you're fishing, eh? Well, you're

one of the youngest men I know, which is only one of the things that make you so attractive. And you're very handsome, and of course the fact that you're incredibly wealthy — '

'Marion, don't joke. I'm deadly serious. I want everyone to know about us, want them to see you with me, want them to see us together. Don't you understand?'

She was silent, unsmiling. Her eyes were veiled, glancing downward at her clasped hands. Finally she said:

'You know we can't.'

'Why not? Because of Cotton? You and I know that you never loved him, and neither of us are fooled as to why you married him. Maybe it seemed to you, then, as if it might work sometime. Oh, I don't blame you, and I don't blame Cotton. He must have loved you, right enough. He'd have been a fool if he didn't. But I do blame the old man for forcing it.'

'Don't, Shep.'

'I've got to. We know that you and Cotton never should have married. He just wasn't the type for a thoroughbred like you. He belonged in a boat, or out on the dunes, or in the woods. He'd have been happy married to anyone who'd have been there when he got ready to come home.'

'Don't, Shep.'

'Marion, it's got to come out. I know why the old man forced Cotton to think about you, why he was always inviting you to the house for dinner and always conniving to throw you two together. It was because he needed you, you and the bonds your father left, in his corner for his fight with the bondholders. He would have gone down without you. Believe me, I'm one of the bondholders and I know.'

'Perhaps I knew it too.'

'You?' He laughed bitterly. 'How old were you then? Nineteen, twenty? What could you have known about the sort of man your father-in-law was? Damn it, I'm making an awful botch of this. I'd better give it to you straight. Marion, I want you to be my wife. I want to marry you.'

She lifted her head, startled. 'What are you saying?'

'I want you to marry me.'

She sat a moment, watching him, an unfathomable light in her eyes. Then she turned away to look at the dark water.

'But we can't.'

'We can, after this mess is cleared away. Damn it, it's been five months now. The Navy Department is bound to declare him dead in another month or so. It isn't as if there were some question about it. They saw his plane go down in flames. Nobody got out. You don't just walk away from that kind.'

'But suppose he did come back?'

'In heaven's name, Marion!'

She turned. Her face was white and strained, and in her eyes was a light of hardness he had not before seen.

'Suppose he came back,' she said quietly. 'The Navy found a man on Guam who had been declared dead for more than two years. Almost every week you read of such things in the newspapers. Suppose he came back and was badly hurt, perhaps crippled, and needed me?'

He was silent.

She said, 'Oh, I know you are thinking that it's strange for me, entangled with you in this affair, to be talking about such lofty things as duty and honour and marriage vows. I thought of those things months ago, Shep, and made my choice when I first knew that you and I would travel this road together. You have been thinking that I don't know you very well; perhaps it is the other way round. Does it shock you to know that in my way I am just as selfish as you are? I had a purpose in marrying Cotton, just as his father had a purpose in encouraging him to marry me. I had learned what it was to sit in the big house on Mizzen Hill, shivering with cold because I couldn't pay the oil bill. I had learned how it felt to smile at the butcher all the while he was reminding me of the alarming size of my bill, and what it meant to have the bank of which my father was once president call to tell me that my account was overdrawn. You see, I had been through all that, and I swore it would never happen to me again. And it never will happen to me again.'

'Damn it all, Marion,' he protested. 'If it's security you're worrying about, I've still got enough money to live comfortably on. I may not be as rich as the old man, but . . .'

Her fingers pressed against his lips.

'You don't understand, do you? Let's drop it, shall we?'

He reached out to capture her hand. Doggedly he said: 'Just the same, I'm going to do something about it. There's one of the old Andover boys, Chris Speakman. Should've thought of him before. Chris is way up in the Navy Department. I'll be in Washington next Monday, on business, and I'll drop in to see Chris. He's in a position to put pressure on this thing and get it cleared up in a hurry.'

She pulled her hand away and sat stiffly erect. 'You wouldn't do that.'

'Why not?' he demanded hotly. 'Because of the old man? Marion, be sensible! What is it to you how soon he learns the truth? He'll know eventually, if he lives long enough. You don't owe him anything. I know him, and I know what you're going through, all alone in that house with him.'

'I don't want you to do this thing, Shep,' she said, and her voice contained a quality he had not heard before.

He slid his arm about her shoulders, lifting his free hand to caress her cheek. 'You're a thoroughbred, Marion,' he said huskily, 'and I respect you for it. But just you leave it to Shep, and forget about the whole thing. I'm sorry I've been such a dud tonight, sweet. I feel a perfect rotter for saying so much, but it just had to come out. Maybe you've forgotten, but I asked you to marry me.'

For a moment, it seemed that she would yield. 'I haven't forgotten,' she said. And then she uttered a little gasping breath, and her eyes widened as she stared beyond him.

'What is it?' he demanded sharply, sitting back and jerking his head around. 'Did you see someone out there?'

'I might have. I can't be sure. It's so awfully dark — I thought something moved.'

His eyes groped beyond the glass of the window, and his lips tightened. His hand went to the door latch, and with forced calm he said, 'Reach in the glove compartment. I've a flashlight, and my pistol should be in there. I think I'll have a look around.'

She obeyed, opening the panel and searching swiftly.

'There's a flashlight, but I can't find a pistol,' she whispered. Turning, her hand sought his arm. 'Oh, I'm so frightened! Take me home at once, please.'

He hesitated before closing the glove compartment. Then: 'Guess maybe you're right. I'll take you home.'

Despite his brave show, there was considerable relief in his voice.

The Packard's lights brought the beach and rocks into sudden bold relief. Under his foot, the engine ground into pulsating life, and as they backed away swiftly the headlights bathed dunes, beach and rocks in a searching glow that revealed nothing.

His features relaxed in a smile. 'It was probably just a trick of your imagination.'

She was silent, and as they drove past Frederick Thorne's dark studio, she turned to glance at it speculatively.

★　★　★

Thorne parked his station wagon in the spacious side yard, cut out lights and engine and frowningly contemplated the looming silhouette of the Kendall mansion. On the second storey, light filtered from a shaded window, and below a faint reflection gave evidence that somewhere on the ground floor someone had anticipated his coming.

He let himself out into the bitter night, and as he limped toward the broad stone front steps, the thought came to him that he might very well be making a fool of himself. But the die was cast, and as he mounted to the wide veranda and saw light shining from the narrow glass panels about the graceful entrance, he lifted the heavy brass knocker and brought it sharply down.

Almost at once he was admitted by the housekeeper, a tiny dried-up old woman whose flannel nightgown was supplemented by a tightly clutched bathrobe. Expecting, argument he was agreeably surprised.

'I told him,' she said, sounding perplexed, 'and he said you were to come up. You'll find him in the room at the head of the stairs. Please don't stay long. Doctor Swayle's given strict orders. Mr. Kendall's a terrible sick man.'

Slowly he negotiated the stairs. As his head came above the landing he saw a crack of light beneath the door directly ahead, and making for it he knocked diffidently.

An irascible voice called, 'Come in!' and as he opened the door he heard with increasing volume, 'I've been expecting you since morning. Where the devil have you — '

The voice stopped, and Thorne came face to face with the old man in his bed, propped up by pillows, covers pulled high on his skinny chest. His faded blue eyes darkened and the loose greyish skin on his forehead wrinkled in annoyance.

'Oh, it's you,' he said sourly. 'What the devil do you want?'

Thorne moved into the centre of the room and said stiffly: 'I had no desire to annoy you, Mr. Kendall, and I'm really sorry to disturb you in this manner, but I thought it necessary. What I have to say is important and confidential. I wanted it to be for your ears alone, and that is why I risked coming here.'

The old man turned his grey head, peering in sardonic mockery.

'What in hell could you have to say to me that's so damned important?' he asked.

'I wanted you to know that your son was in my studio. Tonight. I talked with him for nearly an hour.'

The old man closed his eyes. For a moment Thorne was afraid. He hadn't wanted to plunge like this, but the mockery and sarcasm had crumbled all his vaguely formed plans of approach. Anxiously he waited while seconds dropped noiselessly from the sweep-hand of the electric clock on the bedside table. And then the movement of bed-clothing on the skinny chest resumed a regular rise and fall, and the grey old hands moved. The old man opened his eyes.

The artist breathed out. 'Cotton is in pretty bad shape,' he said. 'I wasn't able to learn his exact status. Until we do learn it, I feel that his return should be kept in the strictest confidence.'

'I don't see why I should have any trouble now,' the old man said in a tired voice, 'since I've managed to keep it in confidence for the past two months.'

'Two months!' Thorne gasped. 'Do you mean that he — that you — '

'Sit down,' the old man said, 'and take off your coat. Since you've put yourself into this thing, we'll have to have a little talk.'

Gropingly, Thorne removed his coat and seated himself.

'I don't understand this,' he said dazedly. 'So far as I knew, and so far as you have let everyone believe, until he appeared in my studio tonight, Cotton was missing in action. There hadn't been much hope, and so when I learned of his presence I was nearly overcome. And when he left the studio I sat struggling within myself, my loyalty to him against my reason — '

'You artists make me tired. Sentimental, impractical, always tearing around with a lot of half-baked ideas about trying to help people. So you saw him and he was all smashed up, and your heart went out to him. You probably listened to some crazy scheme of his, all mixed up with ideals and not wanting to hurt people or be a burden. And he doesn't want to come home until he thinks he can make it under his own power.' The old man's jaw shot out. 'Isn't that the general idea?'

'Let's forget my motives.' The artist's bony knuckles showed white. 'As for Cotton's, you've probably stated them correctly, albeit callously.'

'Good.'

The old man pushed bed-covers down, swung his skinny legs around and put his feet into slippers. When he stood, swaying a little, an old-fashioned nightgown ballooned around him. He was sick, and evidently very weak, but he wanted no help. He walked to the wall, pushed aside a framed lithograph of a full-rigged ship, and opened a wall safe hidden behind it. Taking out a sheaf of papers, he carried them with him and returned to bed.

'These,' he said, 'are reports. Everything's here, from the original telegram of notification from the Commandant of the

Marine Corps through the notice of rescue, the reports of his progress in various Naval hospitals, and included are the reports of the male nurse I hired to accompany him from San Diego here. Last night DeSylvia, the nurse, telephoned me from New Haven that he would be here with my son early this morning. But today there was a slight change in plans. It was DeSylvia I was expecting when you appeared.'

Thorne regarded the old man with bleakly hostile eyes. Of the multitude of questions in his mind, only one at last found expression.

'Does Marion know?' he asked.

'She does now.'

'And I came here in confidence, thinking I was the only one who knew.'

'Hunh! Hadn't it occurred to you that a seriously injured man would have difficulty in leaving a war zone, crossing an ocean patrolled by the largest Navy in the world and entering this country in war-time, thereby covering some eight thousand miles, all without the knowledge of the military and naval authorities?'

Thorne stiffened. 'I had thought about

it. Now that you've returned it to my attention, what do you mean when you say that Marion knows 'now'? Why didn't she know before? The military is always extremely careful about notifying he next of kin, especially so in cases such as this.'

'If you are intimating,' the old man said dryly, 'that I have been tampering with my daughter-in-law's mail, you are in error. As a matter of fact, if she did know, it's because the reverse is true. In the confidential statement located in Cotton's personal file, he requested that I be the sole recipient of any information in case of death or serious injury. He further expressly stated that I was to relay that information, at my own discretion, to his wife and other relatives and friends. I believe the process is sentimentally known as 'softening the blow'.'

'And your reasons for withholding this information?'

'I'm not on trial! You yourself came here requesting confidence. You say that you saw Cotton tonight. Are you positive it was him in your studio?'

'I did not actually see him. He stood

behind a screen all the while he was talking. He objected violently every time I made a move, apparently fearing that I would attempt a glimpse of him.'

'Then how are you so positive of his identity?'

'From the things he said. Things from the past, when he was a young lad and I was first starting to paint. Intimate things that would be known only to the two of us.'

The old man's face lost its hostility and became thoughtful. His fingers drummed on the bedside table. 'Yes — yes, it is possible,' he murmured.

It was Thorne's moment for sarcasm. 'You have the notices, and you hired a man to accompany him home. Why should there be any doubt in your mind as to his identity?'

'I built my business by making sure I was right before I proceeded. The Marine Corps, like many another organization, depends principally upon fingerprints for identification. In this instance, the hands and fingers had been badly burned, and the new skin that grew was so filled with scar tissue as to make prints unreliable. Then came the dental records; bridges, fillings and inlays. Worthless because Cotton was one of the few having perfect teeth.' The old man paused and said, 'Another of the few was Sergeant William Stanczyk, the gunner who went down with Cotton in the crash.'

'Stanczyk? Are you suggesting that he would try to pass himself off as your son? Preposterous!'

'Is it? I am not sentimental. I'm hard-headed, realistic and not too honest. If I were a boy who had worked in a mill and one day found myself the survivor of a crash in which the mill-owner's only son had perished, and I knew that my appearance had so changed as to make recognition difficult if not impossible, I might be tempted to play the game.'

'The idea is insane!'

'Consider the stakes, Mr. Thorne. I am worth a great deal of money, and every penny of it goes to my son, if living, and to my daughter if he should precede me in death.'

'He'd never get away with it. There are

means of positive identification other than fingerprints and teeth. The colour and texture of hair and skin; bone structure; shape of the head, hands and feet; width and set of the shoulders; length of neck, arms and legs; colour, shape and spacing of the eyes; shape, size and set of the ears — '

'Very true. But you didn't see him. When the natives delivered him to the boat that brought him off the island, his outfit had moved north with the combat zone. At that time he appeared to be suffering from amnesia; there was no one on hand to identify him. The only claim he had to being Lieutenant Kendall was possession of a dog-tag which he might easily have secured from the wreckage of the plane while he was recovering.'

Thorne's bony fingers tugged at his yellow hair. 'He may have been suffering from amnesia then, but he certainly isn't now. Whether you want to believe it or not, the man in my studio tonight was your son. Physically and mentally, he is in deplorable condition. He is facing some-thing bigger and tougher than his fighting in the Pacific ever was, and it's a battle he's got to win before he can face you or me or his wife or anyone.'

Tiredly the Old man said: 'I suppose that damned DeSylvia is looking all over hell for him, too scared to telephone me — ' He raised the covers and eased his legs off the bed again. 'Did Cotton tell you where he was staying?'

'No.'

'Was he in need of money?'

Thorne hesitated. He hadn't told the old man the apparent purpose of Cotton Kendall's visit, to secure the pastel head for a pattern a surgeon might use. That, Thorne supposed, would be seized upon by the old man as prime evidence in support of his suspicions.

'No. Apparently he had enough.'

The old man walked in a weaving line to the safe, thrust the papers inside, closed and locked it and replaced the framed lithograph. Then he shuffled back to bed.

'No doubt he'll be coming back to see you. If you should give him any money, you will be reimbursed. I'll appreciate reports on his progress, and I am deeply grateful to you for coming here tonight. Good night, and thank you.'

'Let's get one thing clear,' Thorne said, rising. 'You couldn't have had any suspicions as to Cotton's identity, not in the beginning. You would have been tremendously relieved to get the notice of rescue. And you wouldn't have questioned the authenticity of the sole survivor because at that time you probably wouldn't have known that there was only one survivor. I would like to know why you didn't tell Marion then.'

'I had my reasons.'

'What possible reasons could there have been?'

The old man sat up and the covers fell away, leaving the nightgown to sag against his skinny chest. His eyes were old and very tired.

'I told you before that I'm not on trial. That boy is my only son, and he means more to me than anything on this earth or in the heaven hereafter. Even more than my first-born, my daughter Prudence, his half-sister. Everything I've done or planned or built has been for him. He meant so much to me that, although I was lonely after his mother's death in Nineteen Thirty, I did not marry again because of his devotion to her memory.

'I have been grateful to you, although I have never expressed my gratitude because such things do not come easily to me. I am grateful because you helped Cotton fill the gap caused by the death of his mother. You gave him something that I could not, and I am now doubly grateful because you have given me the first real hope I've known in months of doubt and anguish. I want nothing to spoil my gratitude, just as I want nothing to spoil my son's return. In this, I think, my motives may be identical with yours. And so, Mr. Thorne, you must excuse me. I am not a well man.'

The artist nodded, picked up his coat and hat and limped from the room, quietly closing the door. Down the long, difficult stairs he went to the hall below, empty now of its tiny aged guardian. And as he put on his coat, he was conscious of a surging sense of shame for himself and of pity for the tired old man who, like his son, was fighting so desperately and so alone.

In the cold night, Thorne started the station wagon and guided it down the straight drive. He was between stone pillars that marked the entrance to the road when he saw the Packard moving away, and saw that the young woman who had emerged from it was Marion Kendall. She stood a moment, watching the Packard, and then turned and walked briskly along Mizzen Hill Road without apparently noticing him.

'She was with *Ford Sheppard*!' he said under his breath.

Suddenly the whole picture was sharply, brutally clear.

3

Tessie Morgan, struggling between dream and awakening, groaned and brought her arm up to protect her eyes from the morning sun. Dully she wondered what time it might be and whether the ringing she had heard was the alarm clock or the telephone or just a part of the dream.

Whatever the ringing had been, it had stopped. And it was probably late. Mr. Heath would be in a fine humour by the time she reached the office, with all those reports to get out. Well, let him be. She would be in a fine humour herself. What was it she had been drinking? Pink things . . .

Tessie Morgan sat bolt upright in bed and let out a yell.

The broad-shouldered, blockily built and heavy-faced man who was seated not three feet from her said, 'Shut up.'

'Ben Sutts! *Damn* you, you scared me half to *death*. What are you doing, sitting here in my room before I'm out of bed? How long have you been here?'

The blocky man clenched enormous fists. 'Quit your yelling,' he said.

Tessie grabbed a blanket and made a protective shield of it. 'I will *not* quit yelling, and don't *you* holler at me! And get out of here or you'll hear some *real* yelling. Get out. *Get out!*'

Ben Sutts opened his fists slowly.

'I ain't gonna get out, and if you don't quit your yelling I'm gonna strangle you.'

Tessie looked at his eyes, little and hard and flinty grey, and felt a scared sinking in her stomach.

'You lay a hand on me and I'll call the cops,' she blustered. 'What do you want?'

'You know what I want.'

'I most *certainly* do not.' She paused, and her eyes narrowed. 'Say, how did you get in here?'

'You left your door unlocked.'

'I *did* not! You must've climbed up the fire escape. You — you *burglar*! What do you want?'

'You stood me up last night. Not for the first time.'

'I was working,' Tessie said defensively. 'And what of it?'

'You wasn't working. I know where you was. At the Well-House Tavern with some sailor you picked up. Manuel saw you there.'

'Manuel's a dirty liar!' Tessie declared hotly. 'He didn't see me at the Well-House or anyplace else, because I was working. And, besides, I don't see that it's any business of yours. I'm not married to you.'

'Manuel don't lie to me,' Ben Sutts said.

All the time he had been sitting there, he had not moved except to open and close his enormous hands. His small flint-grey eyes had remained fixed in the region of Tessie's throat. He did not move now, or speak further. He just sat, his head sunk slightly forward on his tremendous shoulders, watching her.

A couple of minutes ticked noisily away on Tessie's alarm clock.

Tessie passed rapidly through a confusing series of emotions. First she had come to startled wakefulness. Then there had

73

been swift anger, followed by swifter fear. Now she was feeling somewhat ill.

'Ben, don't just sit there and *stare* at me like that. For God's sake, say something. Say it and go home so's I can get dressed and go to work. I'm an hour late already. Mr. Heath'll *scalp* me!'

Except for his hands, he did not move.

'All right, so I *was* at the Well-House last night. With a sailor. And why? You made me so *damned* mad. You called me up at the office yesterday and you didn't ask me if I was doing anything or did I want to go someplace. You just *told* me to be ready at seven o'clock, that you were going to take me to the movies. What do you think I am, one of your Portuguese fishermen?'

He didn't say.

'You don't own me! Nobody does. So I said to myself, 'All right, Mr. Ben Sutts. Just you go ahead and start taking me for granted, and we'll see.' So I drove in my car down to the Well-House. And I picked up a cute sailor. And he *kissed* me, too. And I liked it. And he wants another date and I told him he could have one. Now, what've you got to say to *that*?'

Ben Sutts said, 'Someday I'm gonna break your damned neck.'

'Try it!' Tessie flared. 'Try it just once, and see what happens! That's all you know, you dumb ox! Threatening people with your *muscles*. Well, if you so much as lay a hand on me you'll regret it as long as you live. If you ever touch me just once, I'll be the last person you'll touch. You — you lousy *pig*! Get out of here. *Get out!*'

Ben Sutts pushed himself slowly from the chair and stood towering above her, his head lost to her view because of the canopy over her bed.

'I'm dumb, all right,' he said slowly. 'I should've known better than take up another man's garbage.'

The nearest thing to her was an ivory and rose bed lamp, small but substantial. Tessie threw it, and the force of her throw disconnected the cord from the base plug and upset the stand it had rested on. The cord spoiled the aim, but it didn't spoil the effect.

For an instant, Ben Sutts seemed to

swell. And then in fearsome contrast to his slow speech, he moved with lightning speed. Grabbing the blanket, he cleared it from the bed with a single vicious yank that threatened to tear away Tessie's tightly clenched fist. His great hands scooped her up, dislodging the canopy in the process. She was kicking and clawing and trying to bite him, but she wasn't doing so well.

Turning her over, he administered a series of swift, shattering blows upon her unprotected back. And then he dumped her, a frothing, furious heap, on the bed.

Ben Sutts lumbered to the red-enamelled door and there paused to adjust his coat with an outward movement of his heavy shoulders and tremendous arms. Presenting Tessie with a baleful glare, he spat disdainfully on her carpet.

'Suppose you tell your high and mighty friends and your sailor pal, the cops, and everybody else around Sudwich that you've laid with,' he said, 'suppose you tell them Ben Sutts put a hand on you.'

'I'll tell them! And I'll tell them plenty! About you smuggling on the *Tessie M*, and selling short lobsters and poaching on Townsend's pots and stealing petrol from the Navy barge, and that knife fight . . . '

Ben Sutts came back a little way into the room. He was ominously quiet.

'I don't think you will,' he said in his slow, stumbling voice.

He stood a moment, watching her, and then strode from the room.

★ ★ ★

Ford Sheppard was practising chip shots on his lawn with his favourite five-iron when Henry Heath's Cadillac swung into the drive. The Cadillac slid to a stop on the gravel surface, and Sheppard expertly chipped a ball over the hood and onto a brown patch of grass beyond.

The alarm in Heath's eyes changed to admiration. 'Beautifully done,' he sighed.

Sheppard grinned. 'It's all in the wrists, m'boy. What brings you out this early of a frosty morning? How about coming in for a drink?'

'I — well, all right.'

They entered the living-room by way of a comfortable glassed-in porch. Beneath a graceful mantel, a log fire burned.

Indicating a brocaded barrel-back chair, Sheppard said: 'Sit down. Won't be a moment. The help are at market, battling with Kessler and coupons as usual.'

Henry Heath sat and glanced enviously at the evidence of wealth displayed around him. The expensive Persian rug, and the genuine period furniture. And the paintings: there was one of Frederick Thorne's which he knew, because he had inquired about it at the Sudwich gallery, had cost thirty-five hundred dollars.

Yes, Ford Sheppard certainly spent money lavishly. Of course he'd inherited a potful from his father. And he should have a lot of it left — Henry Heath's eyes gleamed with cupidity. It would suit his purposes to find out just how much.

Sheppard came in, bearing a tray. 'Name it,' he said.

'Scotch and water. No ice.'

'Smart drinker. Here, pour your own.'

They served themselves and settled down.

'Um, good,' Sheppard said. 'Now, what's on your mind?'

'The date, for one thing. It's Thursday

the twenty-first of March.'

Sheppard drank, lowered his glass and smiled at it pleasantly. 'Nice of you to come around and tell me the date. Now that that's settled, what's it all about?'

'It seems that I owe you a little matter of eight thousand, and it's due today.'

'Oh! Imagine in this age someone owing you money and dropping around to remind you of it! I guess it's a good thing. Probably got your note someplace — safe deposit box, I suppose.'

'It isn't a note,' Heath said. 'It's a mortgage. On my house.'

'Oh, to be sure. Good investment. Six percent's damned hard to get these days.'

'I have a cheque for the interest here. Two hundred and forty dollars.'

'Well — thanks! Nice of you, right on the dot and all that. They say a mortgage is no better than the character of the man.' Heath coughed and reached for his drink.

'Thanks for the compliment. The point is, I'm a bit strapped at the moment and hope it will be all right to continue with the mortgage open for, say, another year.'

'Open?' Ford Sheppard frowned. 'Well, why not make a small payment on it, say a thousand, and recast it for another five years? Not that your place isn't worth the mortgage, but I like to keep things on a business-like basis, y'know.'

Tiny globes of perspiration appeared on Heath's fat neck. 'I suppose I could pay you something,' he said carelessly, 'but it would mean I'd have to disturb my investments. I'd much prefer to let it go until the year-end, at least. As a matter of fact, I'm in the market for money. A lot of it.'

Sheppard gave him a quick glance. 'Anything wrong? You haven't been speculating with the firm's money?'

'That wouldn't be smart, would it? Me being the son-in-law. No, I know better than to cut my own throat.'

'If Cotton never comes back, you'll be in a pretty good position, won't you?'

'I'm in a good position now.'

Sheppard poured himself another drink and looked at his guest. 'Look here, old man. We're friends. I don't want you to take offence, but for your own good, just how far has this Morgan wench got her hooks into you?'

Red flooded Heath's fleshy cheeks. 'Tessie?' he gasped. 'Who's been giving you that — that drivel?'

'It's pretty common knowledge that you set her up in the apartment over Kessler's store. It's none of my business and I can't say as I blame you. But it does seem to me you're playing too close to home — she's mixed up with some disreputable characters. That Sutts, for one. He's altogether bad.'

Heath gulped down the remainder of his drink. Earnestly he said: 'I'm mighty glad you told me this, and I think I can understand how it started. We picked Tessie out of the mill, gave her a break; I suppose any other woman we'd have picked, the same sort of thing would have happened. You know this town. I've been in Tessie's apartment exactly twice; once when she insisted that I see it, and the second time to pick up some letters she had taken home to type on her portable. I suppose I was foolish to go near the place; but, damn it, as to Tessie having her hooks into me, that's a pile of rubbish!'

'What about that scene with her in front of the post office yesterday morning?'

Heath groaned. 'I might have known that would get around, with Reba and Julie Johnson barging past at the worst possible time. I dumped a load of mail on Tessie, and she spilled polish all over herself. You can imagine how she acted. I hope to goodness Prue hasn't heard about it.'

'You've got to be careful with her. She's an ambitious, designing wench, and a mighty pretty one too.' Sheppard gave him a shrewd glance. 'We still haven't settled the mortgage question. Mind telling me why you're in the money market?'

Relieved at the change of subject, Heath mopped his neck. Settling down, he pursed his lips and swiftly probed his host from bright little eyes. Heath knew things about Ford Sheppard, things which, added to the fact that Sheppard might still have a lot of money, made an interesting total.

'No love lost between you and the old man, is there?' he asked casually.

'Truthfully, no. You know damned well he cost me a small fortune during that bondholder fight. What has that to do with your wanting money?'

'It might have a lot to do with it,' Heath said calmly.

'Look here, I don't know what's in that sly brain of yours, but if it has to do with making money and you're leading up to a proposition, the way I stand with Kendall wouldn't have any bearing.'

'In other words, you wouldn't be averse to making a little at the old man's expense?'

'Legitimately?'

'Yes.'

Sheppard sat up. 'If you've figured out a way, you've done better than I have, and I've been trying for fifteen years.'

Heath chuckled. 'Suppose I told you we could cut thirty thousand apiece from him within the next six months, and he couldn't stop us?'

'He won't live six months. How much do I have to put up?'

'Forty thousand. I'll give you a note for my half. In six months, you'll have your forty thousand back plus thirty thousand profit and six percent interest on my note.'

Sheppard narrowed his eyes. 'That's a lot of money. It'll have to be pretty good.'

'It is. You recall that issue of preferred he put out when he was having all that trouble with you?'

'I ought to. The preferred was what stopped me. Even had to take some of the damned stuff in lieu of interest on the bonds. Seems to me it's passed some dividends.'

'It has, and as a result people have been trying to unload. Because he's sick, they think the mill's going to pot. Naturally, that's knocked the price down. I've been buying it up, here and there. And I've got a wad of it tied up in options, in dummy names. Now I want to move fast before anyone gets wise to what I'm up to.'

'Doesn't sound like such a hot deal to me. If there isn't any market, how can we get our money back?'

Heath leaned forward, smiling faintly.

'We are refinancing the bonds at lower interest,' he said. 'A part of the deal includes retiring the preferred at the call price, one hundred and ten. My options are at forty.' He reached out a fat hand

and gave Sheppard's knee a push, and he leaned back, smiling triumphantly.

Behind his responding grin, Sheppard's eyes were hard. 'Forty thousand means a thousand shares. That adds up to seventy thousand profit. You said something about thirty thousand apiece. What about the other ten?'

'I have to cut in the man who has been doing the legwork, seeing the various people and getting them signed up. And I've got to move fast now. The options start to expire within the next ten days.'

Sheppard frowned thoughtfully. 'You're a damned shrewd operator, and it looks like you've got something. But I'll have to think it over. Not sure I can raise that much on short notice. I'll sound out Finch on what arrangements can be made. Let you know my decision sometime today.'

Heath's eyes clouded. 'You won't let Finch know why you want the money? He's Marion's brother-in-law, you know, and I'm not sure he can be trusted.'

Sheppard grinned. 'I can handle Finch. I own the mortgage on his mother's place, and he'd sell his soul to lift it.

Especially since it's in arrears.'

Heath nodded. 'Maybe so, but don't trust him too far. I've been working on this a long time, and I wouldn't want some slip to spoil it now.'

★ ★ ★

Henry Heath had been gone for perhaps a half-hour when Sheppard's 'help' returned from market. Ford was in the butler's pantry, checking over his supply of Scotch, and so it was quite by accident that he overheard the details of what had taken place that morning in the apartment above Kessler's store.

' . . . and the language they used. My lands!'

'Simply shockin'. A woman like that Tessie Morgan ought to be run out of town on a rail.'

'That she should, but my lands, Ben Sutts ain't no angel. I recall the time he was a boy, when he stole Ford's boat. He was always gettin' into trouble. But I was beginnin' to think he'd made somethin' of himself.'

'Not if he keeps on with that Morgan woman, he won't. Didja hear the racket? He must've beat her. That was right after she called him a 'lousy pig'.'

'E-lizabeth! My lands . . . '

Ford Sheppard stood up, quietly closed the cupboard door and tiptoed from the pantry. His eyes held a light of exultation as he crossed the hall and entered his study. Closing the door, he locked it and reached for the telephone.

After a brief delay, a suspicious voice asked, 'Who's this?'

'Tessie? Ford Sheppard . . . yes . . . please don't sound so shocked. After all these months I thought it was time I apologized. Will you have lunch with me . . . ? Good! I'll drop by at noon. And say, if you should see Heath, don't . . . Oh, you're not working today? Good! We can go for a little drive after lunch . . . Good! 'Bye!'

Convinced that he had never sounded more sincerely penitent in his life, Sheppard grinned and rubbed his hands in satisfaction.

'What a break,' he breathed. 'In fact, two perfectly marvellous breaks. Now, if I can just bring Finch to terms, this'll be the biggest day I've had in years.'

★ ★ ★

Lieutenant Joseph Marshall Dickerson was seated at his desk contemplating some important files when the telephone rang. The files comprised a stack of consecutively arranged newspapers, and his attention was painstakingly centred on the more recent details in the eventful life of his fellow criminal nemesis and idol, Dick Tracy, and so he ignored the telephone.

But the telephone rang again, a loud and annoyingly insistent clamour. He sighed, glancing in perplexity at the fourth and by far the most disturbing panel of the uppermost strip, and divided the telephone in parts.

'Dickerson,' he said.

'Lieutenant? This is Doctor Martens, of the Swann Clinic.'

Dickerson frowned. 'Yes, Doctor. What can I do for you?'

'I realize you must be busy,' the

beautifully modulated voice said, 'but would it be possible for you to drop by the hospital? I would like very much to see you.'

Martens. A plastic surgeon, and a good one. Also something of an amateur criminologist, although he'd been decent enough not to annoy Homicide, up to now.

'I *am* rather busy,' Dickerson admitted. 'Isn't it something you could tell me over the phone?'

'Not with complete justice. I promise not to take up much of your time.'

Dickerson's gaze turned sadly downward to his pile of precious newspapers.

'Well . . . '

'You'll be over? Excellent! Please come as quickly as you can. I have some surgery scheduled for eleven-thirty. Goodbye!'

The large man with the greying temples returned his telephone to its holder. It had started out to be such a promising day! Not a thing on the docket and nothing hanging fire. Sighing, he pushed himself to his feet and returned the newspapers to the battered green steel locker, already crammed with other carefully preserved journals.

Coming back to the desk, he held his thumb on the interphone button and growled: 'I'm going out for an hour. Switch any calls to Connelly.'

'Okay, chief.'

'And tell the rheumatic Civil War vet who allegedly cleans this floor that there's an office behind the pebbled-glass door in Homicide.'

'Okay, chief.'

'And for the umpteenth time this month, quit calling me *chief*!'

'Okay — Lieutenant.'

★ ★ ★

Standing at attention, Joe Dickerson held his hat in his hands and admired the broad, clean expanse of a mahogany desk and the white-robed, white-haired aristocratic man busily engaged in writing there.

'You wanted to see me, Doctor?' Dickerson asked.

Julian Martens glanced up quickly and

smiled. Rising, he came around the desk and extended his hand.

'Lieutenant Dickerson!' he said. 'I recognized you from your pictures. I've followed your work with great admiration. Won't you sit down?'

'Thank you, sir.'

Julian Martens re-seated himself at the desk and turned his swivel chair until he was facing Dickerson.

'Now, first, my reason for calling you. You'll understand that a man in my profession must be careful. All kinds of people come to us wishing to be — er — transformed. In my own practice, I have long made it a rule to investigate rigidly the background of every prospective patient.'

'A very good reason why we've never met before, Doctor.' Dickerson smiled.

'Exactly. Too many people come to me wishing to have their features altered for reasons that are obviously illegal. As a result, we have been forced to maintain a minor criminology department. And that brings me to the case in point. I have been visited by a man who desires to be a patient. Suffice it to say that in his present state, he is one of the most pitiable human objects I have ever seen. At first glance, I would have thought him to be at least in his fifties. But there are certain reliable indices in the human body from which an accurate estimate of age may be drawn.

'One is to be found in the eye. A white line begins to form around the pupil in the early and middle thirties. Although this man's hair was nearly as white as my own, the most cursory examination of his pupils showed him to be under thirty-five. And his almost perfect teeth indicated that he was well under thirty, probably not more than twenty-five or twenty-six years of age. I was intrigued.'

Martens paused, his forehead wrinkled in thought.

'Accompanying him here was a short, muscular and altogether disreputable-looking man who claimed to be a male nurse, gave his name as Carlos DeSylvia and his address, vaguely, as 'just New Haven'.

'Now, I usually interview prospective patients alone, especially if they are brought here by physicians, nurses or members of the immediate family. Frequently there exists an inhibition which may tend to destroy confidence in the interviewer. Thus, while DeSylvia waited in the anteroom — with rather ill grace — I brought the man in here. My first question, name and address, was met with flat silence. That is most unusual.

'Further, all my further questions met with stony silence. I suspected that he might be deaf, and so going behind him clapped my hands together. He jumped and said, 'Don't do that!' His voice was peculiar, indicating that the larynx had at some time suffered severe injury.

'You'll understand,' Martens sighed, 'that his silence placed me in an embarrassing position. I was forced to call in DeSylvia, and upon question the 'nurse' stated that his charge's name was Eugene Cotton Kendall, that he was an injured war veteran and that he had accompanied him all the way from the Naval hospital at San Diego.

'This may well be true, but more important, I believe, is the peculiar mystery surrounding the whole affair. Although he

had refused me even the slightest information about himself — which could conceivably
be laid to amnesia — Kendall's manner
had at first been one of such intense pleading that I was deeply moved. In his eyes
there was so much evidence that his whole
psychological well-being depended upon
the outcome of his visit to me that I felt I
could not definitely refuse to serve him.
But in the presence of DeSylvia, there
came into emergence an entirely new and
alarming personality. Believe me, Lieutenant, I have looked into the eyes of dangerous
men, but when I looked at Kendall I was
both astonished and frightened.'

Martens paused and smiled. 'It is now
time to introduce my — er — exhibit.'

Opening the centre drawer of his desk,
he produced a framed portrait, a pastel of
the head of a youth who at the time of its
making would have been sixteen or
seventeen years of age.

'You may be familiar,' Martens continued, 'with the work of Frederick Thorne,
one of the handful of American artists to
gain international reputation in the past
two decades. Thorne has a studio in

Sudwich, Connecticut, not far from where I once spent my summers before the hurricane unhappily removed my cottage. Thorne's work is most expensive, and it is my understanding that he will do this sort of thing only for an intimate friend. Unfortunately, this work bears no date. But if it is actually what it is represented to be, an earlier portrait of Kendall, then I should judge it was done about eight or nine years ago.'

The surgeon brooded on the pastel head, then shifted his gaze to Dickerson.

'Lieutenant,' he said, 'please don't think me an old lady, but I tell you that I detect here the most dangerous and deceptive depths. His first pleading manner, confused and belied by his utter refusal to answer even the simplest questions about his background; and then, in a moment of incaution, swiftly revealing an infinite and destructive capacity — what would you think if a man of obviously questionable character brought to you a human hulk and then presented you with an exquisite portrait and said to you, in effect, 'Make him to look like this'?

'I cannot accept him as a patient until I know more about him, and yet because of the alarming potentialities of the situation, and the amazing revelation of his hidden character, I cannot just send him away. He returns tomorrow for a definite answer, and that,' the surgeon sighed, 'is why I have called you.'

Dickerson had sat in absorbed silence, occasionally worrying his moustache. Indicating the pastel he said: 'So this DeSylvia wants you to remodel the scarecrow to look like that portrait.'

'Which, alas, is beyond my power to do. I can alter, yes. I can assist Nature in the healing process. I can even perform what some have been kind enough to term miracles. But, make a whole new man to conform to a pattern? I cannot, nor am I sure that I want to. At first, dealing with the man alone, I gathered from his attitude a desire to resume a place in society. But later . . . ' Martens shrugged and spread his hands expressively.

'Might your impression of Kendall be influenced too much by your evident distrust of DeSylvia?'

'Not really. Despite the condition of the so-called Kendall and his reluctance to speak as contrasted with DeSylvia's ready loquaciousness, Kendall is by far the stronger personality of the two. And, I might add, the more dangerous.'

Martens leaned forward in his anxiety.

'Lieutenant, there are many ugly factors here. DeSylvia, who looks like a hired thug; the physically broken yet mentally dangerous charge, who could be any derelict selected from life's scrapheap; and finally, the portrait, evidence that somewhere in the background lies wealth, position and influence. What is the game, and who are the players? I have called on you because of the great facilities at your disposal. You understand? You are interested?'

'I am interested, yes.'

'Thank you. I am convinced that your entrance will prevent a tragedy.'

'Doctor,' Dickerson began carefully, 'I'm a Homicide man, and I'd like to justify my entry into your affairs. The man I work for, the commissioner, is a bit difficult sometimes. He's of the old school, and he has some pretty definite ideas about Homicide's job. If I were to walk into his office and say that I had taken a case because you had read something in a man's eyes ... ' Dickerson shook his head. 'Frankly, sir, the commissioner would laugh me off the force.'

Julian Martens flushed. 'I see,' he said.

Dickerson arose. 'But that doesn't prevent me from taking an interest, and possibly even an unofficial hand. I have been told that you are an amateur criminologist. Why don't you go after this thing yourself?'

'My dear Lieutenant, my hobby is criminology, yes. I am presently working on a manuscript concerning the importance of hair and epidermis in crime detection. But it would be too utterly preposterous for me to attempt a case. Where would I find the time? A constant parade of the maimed and the disfigured crosses my threshold. No; much as I might enjoy trading places with you, alas I neither may nor can.'

'I think it only right to warn you,'

Dickerson said, 'if these men are as dangerous as you think them to be, you must be extremely careful. I wouldn't want to be called back here in an official capacity.'

Martens extended his hand. 'Thank you, Lieutenant. Now, tell me. Would you accept this scarecrow as a patient, or would you turn him away?'

'I think your own investigation should decide that for you,' Dickerson said gravely. 'And I think that is all it should decide. Should your 'criminology department' run into something I can lay on the commissioner's desk, I would appreciate a prompt summons. I think you are sufficiently intelligent to understand why.'

The surgeon's eyes twinkled briefly. 'Thank you, Lieutenant,' he said.

★   ★   ★

Ford Sheppard, seated in the locked conference room of the Sudwich First Bank and Trust Company, glanced up from shuffling through a slender sheaf of certificates and said: 'Don't seem to have that Kendall Preferred in this lot. Maybe you've got it there.'

Mr. Finch adjusted his glasses and searched with thin, predatory fingers through a maze of papers. There were bonds, some of them bearers, those untraceable instruments that were as good as cash. And stocks and mortgages and insurance policies and warranty deeds, evidences of the remainder of the accumulated wealth of a generation of acrimonious shrewdness. Mr. Finch's dull brown eyes masked their thoughts. If he owned this, he'd sell it before it became as worthless as this other one; and whatever had induced the son of Maitland Sheppard to buy so much New Haven Common even if it had been last quoted at less than fifty cents per share?

'The Kendall Preferred,' Finch said in his softly apologetic voice. 'Here it is. Five and one-quarter shares. Par value one hundred dollars per share.'

'Good!' Ford Sheppard gave a relieved sigh. 'Now, tell me what it says on the back. In the fine print — just give me the gist.'

Finch adjusted his glasses and followed

the finely printed script with a finger. 'There are two classes of stock, the common and the preferred. Of the common there are one thousand shares authorized to be issued, and of the preferred, two thousand five hundred shares.' Finch glanced up myopically. 'As I recall, the common has always been closely held in the family. There has never been any of it outstanding with the public.'

'Don't I know it,' Sheppard grunted. 'Go on.'

'The preferred stock has preference as to assets and dividends over the common. Dividends are payable quarterly out of surplus earnings as declared by the board of directors and are not cumulative.'

'Not cumulative? Why, the old thief! How'd he ever unload the stuff? It isn't worth the paper it's printed on. All they've got to do is show a loss and it'll never pay dividends. Can't see what he figures he'll gain by buying it up. Wonder if the old man could be pulling a fast one on him, leading him to believe he's going to refinance so's he'll buy it all up, and then he'll really have him by the short hair?'

There were just too many confusing 'he's' and 'him's' in these spoken thoughts for Finch to furnish an intelligent answer. He coughed and said: 'The preferred is callable at any time at one hundred and ten dollars per share, although it has been selling for considerably less than that.'

'Why would he call it in at a hundred and ten when he can pick it up over the counter for forty?'

Finch did not argue the point. 'It also says that if the board of directors should fail to declare dividends in any three consecutive periods, the preferred stock shall have equal voting power with the common then issued and outstanding — '

'*What?* That fat fox! And I was beginning to think he was trying to rig me. Wonder if he thinks he can really get away with it?'

Finch, not knowing who thought they could get away with what, looked dubious, and not desiring to be interrupted every time he opened his mouth, kept his counsel.

'Think of the nerve of the man,

imagining he can swing a million-dollar proposition on a borrowed forty thousand!' Bringing a gold pencil from his pocket, Sheppard seized one of his mortgage certificates and began to scribble on it. Abruptly he looked up and demanded, 'What's my balance?'

Finch reached thin fingers to a mahogany box, pressed a button and said:

'Let me have the figure of Mr. Ford Sheppard's balance as of this morning.'

There was a brief delay, in which the click of accounting machines was audible. Then the mahogany box responded: 'Two thousand nine hundred twenty-six dollars forty-seven cents.'

'Two thousand!' Ford Sheppard muttered. 'My gosh, is that all? I deposited fifteen hundred only last week. Where in the devil does it go to?'

Finch seized upon the opportunity. 'You really ought to spend some time with your affairs, Mr, Sheppard,' his soft, apologetic voice said. 'There are quite a number of these securities — '

Sheppard waved impatiently.

'Later. Dig me something out of this

junk that the bank'll loan forty thousand on. Give me something to sign and have the cash ready at three o'clock. I'll pick it up then.'

Finch coughed. 'I'm sorry, Mr. Sheppard, but I'm afraid I won't be able to do it for you quite so quickly as all that.'

'What's the matter?' Sheppard asked thickly. 'Mean to tell me there isn't forty thousand worth in all that stuff?'

'On the contrary. It's worth a great deal more than that. But I am not empowered to grant loans for more than ten thousand, even on sound security such as Governments. It would have to be brought before the board, and they do not meet until next Wednesday.'

'*Wednesday?* My gosh, man, I can't wait that long! What's the limit you can loan?'

'Ten thousand.'

'Ten — ' Sheppard stared at the myopic little cashier, and abruptly his manner became wheedling. 'Look here, Finch. You know I'm good for it. I've got a deal on in which I stand to make a hell of a lot of money. If it goes through, you'll be

104

amply repaid. I hold the mortgage on your mother's place, and if you work with me I'll tear it up. Now, how about it?'

'Well,' Finch said nervously, 'I might be able to let you have twenty. I think I could justify it on a two-for-one collateral basis.' He stopped fidgeting and became firm. 'But I could never let you have forty without authorization from the board.'

'Well, if that's the best you can do, it'll have to be. Now, I want a couple of financial reports. One on Henry Heath and one on the mill. They needn't be too detailed. I want 'em ready when I pick up the money.'

'The mill — ' Finch changed colour and coughed.

Sheppard cast him a swift glance.

'Look, Finch. You know me. I've lived in Sudwich all my life, and for a good part of it your wife and her sister, Marion Kendall, were my next-door neighbours. They played in my yard when they were kids. Hell, man. It's a cinch somebody's got to look out for Marion's interests. You know yourself that Cotton will never come back, and the old man is on his last legs. Now maybe you'll understand my motives, and why I don't want you to give Heath an inkling of what I'm about. As a matter of fact, the less said the better, and so I don't want you to mention it to anyone. Now, you just take care of the details, and I'll take care of your mother's mortgage. I've got to run. Got a luncheon date I don't want to miss.'

The thin fingers returned to sorting certificates. 'I'll try to have everything ready, Mr. Sheppard,' Finch said in his softly apologetic voice.

4

Frederick Thorne transferred a bundle of brushes from his right hand to his left, and turning, limped a little way from his easel. With a great depth of feeling, he poured forth a mixture of supplication, invective and abuse which was impartially divided between the unimpressed deities of Mount Olympus and the unadorned mortal on his model stand.

Tessie Morgan rose defensively and replied spiritedly: 'I tell you I'm sore, and so would you be, too!'

'Sore? You're not getting sore from that easy pose. All you have to do is rest there. Judas Priest! Day before yesterday, what? You fell asleep! The day before that, you were hungry! And now you're sore! What in heaven's name is wrong with you?'

'I'm — I'm just sore, that's all. How much longer will you be?'

'If you can contrive to hold still for the next fifteen minutes, and the light holds out, I may be able to finish the shawl.'

Tessie resigned and rearranged herself. 'I'll try. Ouch, damn it! That big *lug*!'

Thorne regarded her through narrowed eyelids, nodded, and with his left hand selected a brush. Dipping the brush in alizarin, he touched it to umber and began to paint. His movements were deft, rapid and sure, executed without flourishes but with a certain rhythmic flow that seemed to draw upon his whole being to serve his swift-moving hand.

'Will it be very much longer?'

'Shut up! For heaven's sake, stop jerking!'

'I'm trying. Honestly I am. It's the way I'm lying, on my — on my back. It hurts me something *terrible*!'

Thorne lifted his arms. 'Fifteen minutes! Fifteen years!' In exasperation he jammed his brushes in the cracked pitcher, and glared at her. With obvious effort he controlled himself and said, 'All right, Morgan. We'll put it off until Sunday. I hope that you'll be feeling better by then. If you can arrange to be here early in the morning, I'll make the sacrifice of getting up and we'll finish this thing.'

Tessie groaned a 'Thank you' and pushed herself up from the couch. Groping with her toes, she found furred moccasins and put them on. Then she covered herself with the shawl and stepped down from the stand and came around to where he was waiting and watching her.

'What's wrong with you?' he demanded. 'You're not just getting even with me for being nasty to you yesterday?'

Her eyes came up quickly. 'Oh, no! I — I hurt myself. I didn't go to work at all today. I couldn't have sat through one of Mr. Heath's long-winded dictations for a million dollars. And I had lunch this noon with an awfully nice fellow who wants to help me, and I had a terrible time. I could hardly sit down. I was so *embarrassed*.'

'I'm beginning to understand where it was that you hurt yourself.'

'Please don't laugh. Maybe it sounds funny, but it isn't. I'm scared.'

'Of what? Of an injury? What did you do to yourself?'

'It isn't that.' Suddenly two bright tears

trembled on her lashes and her hand impulsively sought his arm. 'Oh, Mr. Thorne, I'm so scared to go back to my apartment and stay there alone! There's a bad connection in the wiring, and sometimes when I turn on the light, a fuse blows and then it's dark.' Her hand tightened and her voice became thin. 'Please, could I — could I just stay here with you for a couple of nights? I wouldn't be any trouble. I could sleep on the couch. I wouldn't bother you — '

'You, stay *here*?'

'You wouldn't even know I was in the house. I could get your breakfast for you — I'd be at work by the time you got up. And I wouldn't get in your way. I promise. *Please*, Mr. Thorne!'

'It's ridiculous!' Thorne boomed. 'Just because you're afraid of the dark. Why don't you get the landlord to fix the damned wiring? Say, what or who are you afraid of?'

She had begun to sob now. She had drawn her hand from his arm and she stood desperately alone.

'Ben Sutts,' she choked. 'I — oh, we

110

had a terrible fight this morning. And I threatened to tell things on him because he — because he spanked me. And this noon I was still so mad at him I told Ford Sheppard everything about Ben — '

'*Ford Sheppard?*'

'Y-yes. And I told him all about Mr. Heath, too. Oh, I'm such an awful fool when I'm mad. Please let me stay, Mr. Thorne. Please — you don't know Ben. He killed a man once in a knife fight over a lobster deal. Manuel Zella and I are the only ones who know about it — it was all hushed up — '

'You told that to Ford Sheppard? And what did you tell him about Henry Heath?'

'I — I told him that I was Mr. Heath's mistress.'

'Are you?'

'N-no, but he wanted m-me to b-be.'

Frederick Thorne let go a breath of exasperation and jammed his hands deep in the pockets of his corduroy jacket.

'I wish I could feel sorry for you, but you got yourself into this mess. If you are afraid to stay in your apartment, I suggest that you go home to your folks.'

'I — I can't ever go home again.'

'You can call up one of your friends and have her stay with you.'

'But I haven't any friends.'

'I'm sorry. But you definitely cannot stay here.'

Tessie raised her tear-stained face. Her dark eyes, swollen and desperate, held pleadingly on him. Finding no hope, they slowly fell.

'Mr. Thorne,' she asked in a muffled voice, 'would you — would you do something for me? Would you — would you kiss me, just once?'

'By gosh, *no*! Now, get into your clothes and get out of here!'

⋆ ⋆ ⋆

Whilst Tessie Morgan sat huddled by her telephone, trying to think of someone to call for solace and protection, a quarter of a mile distant, in a comfortable house on the slopes of Mizzen Hill, Henry Heath was at dinner. He was preoccupied with problems of his own, and while they did not immediately concern his volatile secretary, somehow she and her perfidious ways kept cropping up in his thoughts.

Just why had Tessie called the office to say that she was sick, and wouldn't be in today? She'd been well enough to have lunch with Ford Sheppard at the Iron Kettle. Heads together, buzzing like a couple of flies in a bottle for almost an hour. What had they been talking about? And what was Ford Sheppard up to, warning him about her in the morning and then taking her out to lunch three hours later? If he had been trying to pump some information out of her about the refinancing plans, everybody in Sudwich would probably know about it by now.

At the opposite end of the table, Prudence Heath separated bluefish from bones and carried a dainty morsel to her mouth. She dabbed at her lips with a napkin. 'Isn't it a shame that bluefish has so many bones? It's so delicious and quite expensive nowadays, too.'

'Um?' Henry Heath blinked in the

uncertain light. 'Oh, bluefish — Yes, frightful mess. But good, though.'

'You're not eating any of yours, dear. Don't you care for it?'

He drank some water. 'Not hungry, particularly. What time is it, anyway?'

'It's half-past seven. Don't you have your watch?'

'No. Left it at Binney's to be adjusted. Running slow. Binney said he'd have it for me in a couple of days.'

She folded her napkin. 'You've been strange lately, dear. You aren't like yourself. Are you worried about something? I hope it isn't the mortgage. I know it's due soon.'

'Um? Oh, the mortgage. Yes. Gave Ford Sheppard the interest this morning. He was to phone me about extending it.' He leaned forward anxiously. 'He hasn't phoned, has he?'

'No one has telephoned here for you today. They very seldom do. Whatever is the matter, dear? Are you ill?'

'No. Got a lot on my mind, that's all.'

She got up and moved around the table to stand by him. She was small, plain and grey-skinned, with placid brown eyes. She was like her father, the lord and master of Sudwich, except that in the process of reproduction a vital, indefinable something had been lost.

Her hand sought the nape of his neck. 'I wish you'd share it with me, dear. We don't seem to be able to talk to each other anymore, not since you've had so much responsibility at the mill. I know how difficult it must be, with Papa sick. Is there something wrong between you and Papa?'

'Don't be childish, Prue. If something were wrong, I'd tell you.'

'Would you?' she questioned softly. 'You hardly tell me anything these days. In some ways you remind me so much of Papa. I used to listen to him make conversation, not knowing what he was saying. He would be there, but his mind would be miles away, going step by step down the long corridors of the mill, checking each machine and loom, always figuring. I got so I hated the mill.

'Papa changed so after Cotton came. I was seven then. I was only four when

Mama died, and Papa was so good to me. We used to play together. He was so much fun until Cotton came.'

That was as near as she ever came to referring to the fact that she'd had a stepmother for the greater part of her life.

Henry Heath was a little afraid of her when she was in this mood. Evasively he said: 'I wonder what can be keeping Ford Sheppard? Maybe I'd better call him.'

'About the mortgage? It seems to me he has a very good investment. But if he insists on his money, I'm sure I can get Papa to help us. If only Papa weren't so terribly ill.' Her fingers followed the close-cropped hair of his neck upward to rest lightly against the back of his head. 'I do wish you'd tell me.'

'There's nothing! Just business details.'

She was silent a moment. Then, 'I detest gossip, dear, but I think you should know. Reba Johnson had lunch at the Iron Kettle today. She told me she couldn't help overhearing your secretary and Ford Sheppard talking about you.'

'*Saying what?*'

'Something that wasn't at all nice. I

didn't want to believe it.'

'Prue, as God is my judge,' he said hoarsely, 'Reba Johnson is a meddling, vicious gossip! Why, only this morning Ford told me there was talk about Tessie and me. I was shocked at first, but it's what you've got to expect when you pull a woman like that off a loom and give her a break.'

'Is she a good secretary?'

'Not very. Few are nowadays. As soon as they get to be fairly proficient, they run off to Washington for more money.' He turned aggressively. 'And besides, it was your father's idea to hire her, not mine.'

'I'm awfully glad you told me, dear. Now we'll have our coffee and pie, and afterwards we'll talk over the best way to handle Miss Tessie Morgan.' And bending down, she kissed his forehead.

Returned to her chair, she was reaching out for the little silver bell when, from the hall, the telephone rang.

He jumped up, jarring the table in his haste. 'I'll answer it.'

He ran from the dining-room. Prudence Heath's eyes clouded as her hand descended on the silver bell. Before its tinkling note had died, the kitchen door swung open.

Without turning, she said, 'We'll have our pie and coffee now, Deliah. And you might cut some of that sharp cheese for Mr. Heath.'

'Yes, Missus Heath.'

'And, Deliah, if you'd like to go to the picture show tonight, after you've finished the dishes, you have my permission.'

'Yessum. Thank you, Missus Heath.'

Her eyes were thoughtful as she listened to the sounds of her house. In the kitchen, Deliah was humming and moving about, and from the hall her husband's part of the conversation came filtering through.

'Meet you *there*, in half an hour,' he was saying guardedly. 'All right, I'll be there . . . of course you can depend on me . . . yes . . . yes . . . '

When the coffee was brought, and Prudence Heath lifted a fragile cup, her hands were visibly trembling.

★ ★ ★

At precisely seven-thirty, the artist's telephone set up still another clamour, one of many at annoyingly regular intervals after the departure of Tessie Morgan. It was so prolonged and insistent that he felt at last forced to retaliate.

He limped from the kitchen into his studio to pick up the telephone. '*Well?*' he growled.

'Boston is calling you, Mr. Thorne. I've been ringing your phone for hours.'

Boston! At least it wasn't Tessie Morgan with her crazy fears. 'All right. Put them on.'

'Go ahead, Boston. Here's your party.'

'Mr. Thorne?' A man's cultured voice. 'This is Julian Martens, of the Swann Clinic. I've been trying to reach you since noon.'

'I never answer the telephone when I'm working. Do I know you?'

'I'm afraid not, although I did have a cottage not far from your studio before the hurricane — er — removed it. You might have heard of me through my work; I'm sure I've heard of you through yours.'

'I see. If it's about a portrait, I couldn't possibly take you on until autumn. I've a heavy schedule, and I am planning to go away as usual for the summer.'

'That's not quite it. I do wish that I could speak to you in person. My request may sound strange, but believe me it is of the utmost importance. Can you recall having made, some eight or ten years ago, an unusually fine pastel head of a youth, a boy who would then have been in his fifteenth or sixteenth year?'

'A pastel?' Thorne stiffened. 'I've made hundreds of pastels. Why do you ask?'

'My work is plastic surgery, and I have been approached by a man who seeks to be a patient. His condition — well, I have been presented a pastel which is yours. It shows him to have been a dark, curly-headed youth with unusually large and luminous eyes, and fine, almost beautiful features. Your work is so accomplished, I am positive that he was a personal friend. Do you remember such a young man?'

'I might,' Thorne said cautiously. 'Why do you ask?'

'I cannot accept him as a patient unless I know something of him; his back-ground, his authentic name. Of himself he would tell me nothing, but there was a man with him who called himself Carlos DeSylvia and claimed to be a male nurse. Frankly, DeSylvia's appearance was not prepossessing, and I formed an instant distrust of the man.'

'What name did this male nurse give you for his patient?'

'Eugene Kendall.'

Apparently Cotton was making no effort to hide his identity in this quarter. 'The name is correct,' Thorne said. 'I do not know any DeSylvia, but the other man I can vouch for. There can be no doubt as to his identity.'

'I see. Can you tell me something of this young man? His background, friends, home, his obligations? Is he married? He will not give me any information whatsoever.'

So, he did not want this Martens to contact his family; he wanted to wait until he saw for himself just what sort of job Martens would do.

Thorne avoided direct answer. 'Do you think you can help him?'

'I'm not sure that I want to. At first I

was moved to intense pity. But suddenly — how shall I say it? — I sensed that somewhere in his background there are dangerous depths; there is a destructive force at work. If I could learn something about him, enabling me to reach his inner personality and expose this thing . . . You see, Mr. Thorne, I am also a psychologist.'

Suddenly Thorne realised there could be only one answer to this unseen surgeon-psychologist's expressed alarm: Cotton had somehow learned the truth about his beautiful and lonely wife.

Thorne said, 'Before I commit myself, I must ask for your confidence.'

'I am a physician. My life is composed of confidences.'

'How long would the operations and convalescence take?'

'Difficult to say — it is not an ordinary case . . . '

'I ask because there are certain matters which must be — arranged before his return home. Could we work together? Could you keep me informed of his progress, and if necessary delay that progress until I could be quite ready for him to return?'

'My dear Mr. Thorne! Should I decide to accept him, his physical and psychological rehabilitation would require many months. If you mean could I keep him under lock and key, the answer is no.'

'Many months? Just how bad is his condition?'

'Frightful!'

Thorne's fingers tightened until his bony knuckles showed white. 'Do — do you know where he is now?'

'He has an appointment with me for tomorrow. I can give him any message you wish.'

'It is no matter. I expect him to visit me tonight, and if so I shall talk with him. There are certain aspects I cannot discuss over the phone, but I may visit you tomorrow. In justice to him and myself, I must ask you to be patient.'

'I shall be happy to co-operate. Thank you for your indulgence, Mr. Thorne. Until tomorrow, then.'

Frederick Thorne cradled the telephone and limped back to the kitchen. What must Martens think? His efforts to learn Cotton Kendall's background had met no better results from this source than from the man himself. Still . . .

Suddenly, he had begun to shake, and his teeth were chattering. Angrily he attempted to shrug it off, and walking purposefully, switched off the bright light overhead, leaving only the circular glow of his fireside lamp. He dropped into his chair and drew out his watch.

Five minutes before eight. It had been half-past eight when he had first become aware of Cotton's presence on the previous night. A half-hour in which to prepare himself . . .

⋆　⋆　⋆

Henry Heath, seated in Sheppard's study, accepted the glass proffered by his host, and leaning back said: 'I was beginning to get worried. I expected a call from you much earlier, and then when I learned you'd had lunch with Tessie — well, I didn't like it.'

'Tessie?' Sheppard grinned as he added water to his Scotch. 'I saw her about another matter. A personal affair. Looking for information about a certain party. No connection with this deal.'

Had it been as simple as all that? Heath wondered. He said: 'You know, I came within an ace of passing you up on this deal. I hadn't really considered you until this morning, when I came here with the mortgage interest.'

'You could have arranged for the money elsewhere, I suppose,' Sheppard said casually.

Heath waved a hand. 'Not too difficult. People with money are always on the lookout for a good thing.'

Sheppard gave him a sideways, crooked grin. 'Maybe I've discovered just what a good thing it is.'

Heath's eyes narrowed. 'If you think there's a catch to this deal, you're wrong. The preferred will be called at a hundred and ten. We can't lose.'

'You mean *you* can't lose. That's about it, isn't it?'

Sweat appeared above Henry Heath's collar. 'If you are implying that I'm trying to rig you, we'll quit now while we're still friends.'

'Oh, no we won't. You can't get me out now. You see, I happen to know what you're up to.'

Heath leaned forward. His fat face had suddenly become a hard mask. 'What am I up to?' he asked quietly.

'You are rigging the preferred stock to gain control of the mill. You haven't the slightest intention of letting it go to call. When you've got the voting control in your pocket, you'll call an extraordinary stockholders' meeting, elect your own board of directors, throw out the financing plans and take over. You'll have the old man by the short hair. You'll be the big frog in the pond, and instead of taking orders as you have for the past twelve years, you'll be giving them. That, my friend, is what you are up to. So I want in.'

'How far in?'

'Fifty percent.'

'For a miserly forty thousand? You're crazy!'

'For less than forty thousand. For twenty. I've got it here, in cash, together with the thing you're to sign making me chairman of the board when you reorganize.'

Heath's face was apoplectic. 'Twenty thousand?' he said hoarsely. 'Now, see here — '

'I said twenty thousand. You won't have any trouble raising the rest.' Sheppard grinned mirthlessly. 'There are plenty of people with money looking for a good thing.'

'And if I refuse?'

'You won't.'

Heath leaned back, pressing his fingertips together. In a calmer voice he said: 'You seem to be pretty sure of yourself. You know, I've spent a lot of time on this. You said something about my taking orders for twelve years. Maybe you've forgotten what I was doing before that. Maybe you don't recall the Heath mill on River Street, the one I had to give up after Kendall ran me into the ground. Oh, he was generous. He gave me a job — even let me marry his daughter. But for more than twelve years I've been working, taking orders and waiting. That's a long time, Sheppard, and it's cost a lot of money. I've invested better than sixty thousand dollars thus far, gathering up that preferred. Now that I'm where I want to be, I don't intend to let you or anyone else stop me.'

Sheppard drained his glass and tabled it. Abruptly he said, 'Heath, you're a fool. Any man's a fool who thinks he can pull this off by himself. You say you've spent sixty thousand. How much d'you think the old man'll spend when he settles down to fight? I don't care how sick he is; he's not sick in the head. And he has it to spend. He'll have you squirming long after he's dead and in the ground.'

'When he finds out what I'm doing, it will be too late.'

'Think so?' Sheppard's eyes held a wicked gleam. 'Suppose I should just telephone him now?'

'You wouldn't do that.'

'Wouldn't I? Why should I gamble twenty thousand for the chairmanship of the board when I can have it free, for just making a telephone call? All I have to do is lift that receiver and say a few appropriate words. And then, my friend, your fat will be in the fire. All twelve working and watching and waiting years of it.'

The fat little man closed his eyes. 'So,' he said.

'Here, don't take it so hard! Have a drink.' Leaning forward, Sheppard touched Henry Heath's knee. 'Listen to me. Don't you see what I'm driving at? Maybe you can pull this off by yourself. But what will you do afterward? How are you going to face your wife and your father-in-law? And what about Cotton, if he should come back? With me in there, you'll have an out. It can be Ford Sheppard who has been scheming for twelve years to get control of the mill. You can be just as surprised as anyone when your proxies elect me chairman of the board. And I'll play ball with you. While people are cussing me for a thieving scoundrel, they'll be upholding you as a good man — Henry!'

Responding to the tone and the pressure on his knee, Heath opened his eyes. 'Yes?' he asked dully.

'You damned fool! Don't you see this is going to take money? Twenty thousand or sixty thousand are only drops in the bucket. We're playing for millions! You could never swing it by yourself. You need me in there to help you.'

Heath pushed himself up slowly, deflated and rather ludicrous. His hands strayed blindly in search of his hat. 'I'll have to think it over.'

'Good man!' Sheppard jumped to his feet and, stepping back swiftly, opened a drawer of his desk. 'I knew you'd see it my way. Here, take this. I don't want it. And remember, there's plenty more where it came from. And, just as a formality, maybe you'd better sign this.'

The fat little man stared blindly at the bundles of hundred-dollar bills in Sheppard's careless hand. His eyes, lustreless and with grey pouches under them, strayed to Sheppard's smiling, confident face.

'No. No! I — I won't do it. I — damn you, let me by. *Let me by!*'

★ ★ ★

Beyond the confines of the studio, the brisk March wind was momentarily stilled, and above the sputter of the log fire came the distant and lonely howling of a dog. And then engulfing the dog's cry was the flat, honking call of the Boston-New York express, held up at the Sudwich station a mile across the bay and whistling for the channel bridge. But of the nearer sounds that Thorne had been straining to hear for more than an hour, there were none.

Suddenly he could endure it no longer. He quickly crossed the studio and opened the door to step out on the brick terrace.

The night was cold and still, and the moon gave a ghostly radiance to the rolling expanse of sand. Across the bay, the town's lights twinkled like earthbound stars, and at the station the locomotive's headlight turned rails to gleaming ribbons and made a black, intricate pattern of the closing channel bridge.

If Cotton had been coming to visit him tonight, he would have followed the tracks and crossed over to the dunes by the railroad bridge; use of the bridge and the railroad right-of-way reduced the walk to and from town by more than two-thirds of its distance. That would be the way he had come last night.

The sudden ringing of his telephone startled him. Re-entering the studio, he crossed swiftly and lifted the instrument.

'Well?' he asked.

He heard a rumbling sound, filled with the hiss of escaping steam and the muted, mechanical note of a bell. And then, a voice he had come to know with immeasurable sadness. 'Maestro, are you alone?'

'I am alone. You are coming?'

'I can't, now. Would it be possible for you to meet me in the square, in front of the bank, in about half an hour? I've got to talk to you. There's something — you'll come? You won't let me down?'

'I'll come at once, if you wish.'

'No — in half an hour. And please be alone. Don't fail me, Ford. I need you.'

'I won't let you down.'

He stood thoughtfully, eyes narrowed, holding the connecting cross-bar down. And then, releasing it, he waited until the operator came on and said calmly, 'Get me the Dunes Club.'

When he got through, the reply to his

question sounded stridently above a background of talk and laughter.

'Ford Sheppard? He isn't here. He generally comes in around eight and leaves before then, but he hasn't been here tonight. Any message?'

'No. No message.'

He put the phone down and then picked it up again to call the number of the Kendall residence. When a brittle, cautious voice responded, he said: 'I'd like to speak to Marion Kendall.'

'Mrs. Kendall?' It was the tiny, aged guardian. 'Why, she left for Boston right after lunch. She might be back on the late train, but she didn't leave any word. You might call again in the morning. You're Mr. Thorne, aren't you?'

'Yes.'

'If she's here in the morning, I'll tell her you called, but I won't be up if she comes in on the late train.'

'Thank you.'

He replaced the phone, frowning in thought. Then he moved to the small table on which stood the carved teakwood box. His face was set in grim lines as he pulled out the table's single drawer and searched through it swiftly. When he straightened, his left hand held a small snub-nosed revolver.

Carefully he broke the barrel, and twirled the cylinder to inspect the six cartridges it contained. Satisfied, he locked it and thrust it in the side pocket of his corduroy jacket.

★　★　★

Ford Sheppard glanced at himself in the rear-vision mirror, ran an approving hand along his grey-templed hair, touched his tie with a final practised tap, and then leaned back against the leather seat to listen to his softly playing radio.

I'll walk alone . . .

The hands of the dashboard clock pointed to five minutes before ten.

Sheppard smiled and thought of what an eventful day this had been. First had come Heath, who had sweated and slaved and connived for twelve weary years to formulate the scheme he had in one fumbling moment dumped into his receptive lap.

134

The Kendall-Sudwich mills. Good for a hundred thousand a year. The same mills that he himself had done plenty of sweating and conniving over, only in the end to find himself beaten by the old man, the master conniver.

But things would be different now.

And Henry Heath? The fat little fox had looked so funny, with all the wind out of him, sitting there and listening to terms. Served the damned fool right, trying to rig his own father-in-law. Where was his sense of loyalty? What if the old man *had* put the Heath mill out of business; hadn't he made him manager of his own mill, with more money in salary than he'd ever made in earnings? Heath was a fool.

Three minutes of ten.

Until you come for me, the radio's soft voice was singing.

What a break that had been, overhearing the talk about the fight between Tessie Morgan and Ben Sutts. And what a further break to find Tessie in such a receptive mood. So Ben Sutts had killed a man, eh? Ben Sutts had a little political power now; he was getting up in the mill and fishing crowd. He was gaining influence, and his influence would come in handy in the turn that things would soon take in Sudwich. And Ben Sutts would have to lick the dirt from Ford Sheppard's shoes.

Two minutes of ten.

In two minutes, the door on the kerbside would open and she would be there, wearing a fox jacket; and with her would be the faint, exciting odour of gardenia. She would be hatless, and her burnished auburn hair would be piled in a mass of tight ringlets above her ears. She would stand a moment, smiling, and in her low and exciting voice would say, 'Hello, I'm in luck! Going my way?'

As he thought of her, his body grew warm. *I must be pretty far gone on her*, he mused. *Asking her to marry me. One of these days I'm apt to say that to the wrong woman, and then I'll be in trouble. Still, I might marry her. I don't suppose she's got two dimes to rub together, but I won't need money if this deal goes through. And she's got plenty of class.*

She's smart and she's cool and she knows what she wants.

His reverie was interrupted by a sound of movement. A darker form materialized in the darkness on the kerbside, and the door handle turned downward.

Smiling, he leaned over. And then the smile froze to a gaping ludicrous mask.

There was a simultaneous flash and shattering roar, and Ford Sheppard dropped forward and down. In the direct centre of his forehead had appeared a neat black hole from which blood pulsed in a steady, widening stream. He had been leaning forward, expecting to close the door.

But the door remained open, and thus, in so far as Ford Sheppard was concerned, it would remain forever.

5

Lieutenant Joseph Dickerson closed the door carefully, stepped to the precise centre of the worn green carpet, stiffened to attention and said: 'Yes, Commissioner?'

The commissioner raised his scowling face from some reports he had been studying, waved a hand as large and hairy as a coconut and said: 'Sit down. You working on anything in particular right now?'

Dickerson pulled a chair nearer to the desk. 'No, sir.'

'Good. I've got an unusual job for you. It's an honour, and the department will be on trial. As you know, we've been working on an idea to swap talent between the law enforcement agencies of the various New England communities. Not to try, you understand, to show the other departments up, but to gain a closer co-operation and effect an exchange of ideas and methods.'

Dickerson understood all right; he'd had a hand in planting the idea. He said: 'It sounds like a very good plan.'

'Yeah. Well, the Connecticut State Police have put in a hurry-call for a man. Matter of fact, they asked expressly for you. You'll draw expense money and you'll make your reports direct to Hartford and to me. You'll have all the co-operation that Hartford and I can give you.'

'It must be something big, sir.'

'It is. You've read the newspaper this morning?'

'Not thoroughly. I was — um — catching up on some back reading. Hadn't arrived at the front page.'

'I'll give you a brief outline, together with suggestions as to how I want you to proceed. First, you are to give everyone you contact the impression that you're a member of the Connecticut State Police. Arrangements have been made to supply you with credentials, and only the man working with you, Sergeant Boyle, will know that you're from Boston Homicide. Second, you'll be extremely careful not to

139

offend either the Connecticut authorities or the local constabulary. Just because you're from a big department, you're not going to pull any fast stuff that will cause dissension or jealousy. And third, if you do succeed in breaking the case, you bow out fast and come back here. No banquets. Understand?'

Dickerson reddened. 'That wasn't my idea, that banquet last year. I didn't even know who it was for until I was in the hall.'

The commissioner waved a hairy hand. 'No matter. Now, the case. Murder. Not one of those two-bit scrapes in which a nobody gets bumped off, but the murder of an outstanding citizen. Ever hear of Ford Sheppard?'

Dickerson worried his moustache. 'Let's see . . . Sort of a playboy, some years back, wasn't he? Always rumoured to be engaged to actresses and the like, but never getting married?'

'That's him. His father managed, before he died, to get control of half the traction companies in New England, and Ford Sheppard has been throwing money around like a drunken sailor ever since. He inherited a partnership in the local brokerage firm of Tyndall, Sheppard and Cambridge, and he was squeezed out a few years back. It's because of the possibility of a local angle that we've been called in.

'Sheppard was a resident of Sudwich, Connecticut, in which town his body was found last night. He had been shot in the head with a single slug. He had been seated in his coupé in a street adjoining the Post Road, one block above the main square. Several people heard the shot, but the first to investigate saw no one near the car. There's more information here which you can study on the train. You're to leave South Station at ten o'clock, and Sergeant Boyle will meet you in Sudwich.'

'Sudwich,' Dickerson said thoughtfully.

'A little mill, fishing and summer art town. Don't know what you can expect to find there, but Boyle will get you a place to stay.'

Dickerson stood up. 'I'll do my best, sir.'

'You'll have to,' the commissioner

chuckled. 'Remember that speech you made last month to the New England conference? About there being no such thing as a 'clueless murder'? Well, it looks like the conference has tossed that speech right back in your lap!'

★   ★   ★

Dickerson had passed through Sudwich many times, travelling as he frequently did between Boston and New York. As his train slowed down for the station now, he saw from the vestibule that the village was built along the bank of a river or bay and extended up the side of a fairly steep hill. There was a sprawling mill on the left-hand side of the tracks, and beyond the mill were sandy wastes, more bay, and a few scattered houses strung along a curving spit of land that bordered the sound.

On the town side the houses were neat, square, and pleasantly set in spacious plots of ground. As he stepped to the platform, Dickerson saw that the station was in an isolated spot. Solidly and drably built of brick, it comprised only a waiting room and Railway Express agency. Between the two, on the covered vestibule-high platform, was a telephone pay-booth.

The waiting room was closed and secured with a padlock, but there was activity in the Express agency. Here a grizzled sweater-clad man was busy with labels, paste and packages. His labours did not cease when Dickerson entered and inquired about access to the waiting room.

'You want to buy a ticket?' the labourer asked. 'You just now got off the train. The town ain't that bad.'

'As a matter of fact, I wanted a timetable.'

'Thought so. If you'd wanted a ticket, I'd've let you in. I'm the ticket agent too. Here's a timetable.' He indicated a wire rack. 'Take one. From Boston, ain't you? Could tell by your talk. Don't see that you need a timetable. There's only three trains a day stops here from Boston: leave South Station ten a.m. — the one you just come on — and seven and ten p.m. Them night trains only stops here to discharge or pick up passengers, so's if you want a night train to New Haven and west, you got to notify the towerman. And there's just two trains to Boston and east from here: leave six-fifteen a.m. and two-fifteen p.m. Easy to remember. Stranger in town?'

Dickerson admitted that he was. 'At what hours are these offices open?'

'The station's open when I'm open. Nine to five. If you want a taxi, call One Hundred. If you want a room, there ain't none. Town's full.'

Dickerson thanked him gravely and returned to the platform to discover that it would not be necessary to summon a taxi, for awaiting him was a uniformed state trooper.

Sergeant Boyle of the Connecticut State Police turned out to be a lean, lantern-jawed and thirtyish individual. He had a pleasant and intelligent if somewhat worried face, and his keen eyes were blue.

'I'm glad you're here,' Boyle said. 'I'm just about beat.'

Dickerson smiled. 'My instructions are that I am to work under you. You know the territory and the people involved. You'll give the orders. I may make suggestions from time to time, but I won't give you any trouble.'

'I don't need any more than I've got,' Boyle said wryly. 'As for your working under me — well, I've heard about you. I'm glad you're here. The car's over here in the parking yard. If you don't mind, we'll get back right away. We can talk while I'm driving.'

They passed by lined-up Railway Express trucks from which boxes imprinted *Kendall-Sudwich Mills* were fast disappearing into the train. They came around the corner of the small brick station and descended steps to a gravelled lot where a Buick station wagon bearing the Connecticut seal and the legend *State Police* was waiting. Boyle had started the engine when he resumed.

'I was lucky enough to arrive within a half-hour of the actual shooting. Bert Westcott, the constable, had the place blocked off, and he'd called the Cataract Hose Company to help him hold the crowd back. He's a good man, Bert is. Nothing had been touched before I got there.' The Buick pulled out into the street. 'On our way I'll drive you past where Sheppard's car was parked. Gosh, Ford Sheppard! I can't get over it.'

'You knew him?'

'I was born here. My dad's a letter carrier. I went to school with Shep, as far as the eighth grade. After that, his dad sent him to Andover. Trouble with Shep was, he had too much money.'

They progressed past a lumber yard and long warehouses and made a turn into the Post Road. A number of neat square houses, a church and a school slipped by, and then the business section appeared. Just before they reached Sudwich Square, The sergeant indicated the post office with a nod.

'My dad has worked there twenty-one years,' he said proudly. 'In all that time he hasn't missed a single day.'

The Buick passed Sudwich Square at a crawling pace and began to climb. Boyle said: 'Look sharp now. On the right is the Sudwich First Bank and Trust Company; remember the location. This building next to it is Johnson's Feed Store, and here is the corner of Liberty Street. I'm going to turn here. Now, that's the place.'

They swung into Liberty Street, and Sergeant Boyle raised a pointing finger only to bring it quickly down.

'Darn 'em!' he scowled. 'You see what I mean about trouble?'

Constable Westcott, a full-stomached, considerably haggard man, was the centre of a knot of citizens. At the kerb was parked a battered Chevrolet sedan, its door swung precariously open, and in it someone was stretched in playful mimicry of death.

Dickerson saw and smiled. His quick smiling eyes dismissed the morbidly curious group and swept on to note the windowless depth of the feed store on the right, the tenantless filling station beyond, and on the left the high flanking ledge of rocks.

'The killer picked a dandy spot,' Dickerson mused, as Boyle angrily twisted the wheel to avoid the too-demonstrative crowd.

★ ★ ★

Sergeant Boyle wouldn't listen to Dickerson's suggestion that they have lunch in a restaurant, not with baked beans — New England style — brown bread, and fresh apple pie at home.

They were down to coffee when Boyle brought out photographs. Boyle's wife, a quiet bright-eyed little woman, forever established herself in Dickerson's esteem by firmly and quietly grasping two small Boyles and piloting them off to elsewhere.

'Not much to give you,' Boyle said. 'At least six different people heard the shot, and all of them put the time at exactly ten o'clock. They all agreed that the chimes of the clock on the bank building had just finished striking when the shot sounded. Most of these witnesses said they thought it was the backfire of a truck, since the hill is quite steep at that point. There is one man, Frederick Thorne, an artist, who was seated in his station wagon in front of the bank, and he distinctly heard the shot and verified the time angle, but he seemed to be confused about the direction from which the sound came. That isn't surprising since the ledge along

Liberty Street acts as a sounding board and throws an echo clear to the river.'

'Frederick Thorne?'

Dickerson's memory opened and he saw an aristocratic white-haired man, distressfully concerned with one of Frederick Thorne's pastel portraits.

'I see you've heard of him. He lives in a studio out on the dunes. He assisted Westcott by going to the fire station to get some men. His testimony wasn't of much help except in establishing the time. But Perry Thompson, a discharged veteran who lives at Number Twenty Liberty, was in the woodshed in back of his house, getting ready to bank the heater for the night. Perry has had too much experience with the sound of firearms to be fooled. He recognized it at once as having been made by a small-calibre weapon, but he wasn't sure of the direction, either. He dropped his load of wood and started down his drive to Liberty Street.

'Now along there by the feed store and the filling station, that street is very dark at night. They depend on light from the square at that end, and the next nearest street light is at the intersection of Mizzen Hill Road, a block in the other direction. Perry was on the pavement trying to figure out where the sound had come from when he noticed a coupé at the kerb next to the ledge. He had several reasons for noticing it: one, that it was the only car on the street; another, because the door on the kerbside was standing open; and last, because he had seen it parked there at night before and as recently as the previous night.

'Perry said it couldn't have been more than a couple of minutes between the time he heard the shot and when he reached the street, but he didn't see anyone standing near the car. He noticed that the coupé's lights were off, and while he could see through the rear window because of the lights from the square, he couldn't see anyone sitting in the coupé. It struck him as strange, so he started up the centre of the street.

'He was about opposite the filling station when he thought he saw movement in the shadow in the rear of the feed store. He had progressed a couple of steps when he heard a shuffling sound, like a rat trying to drag an apple — those were his words. But he didn't go back there to investigate, because by the time he made up his mind about it he had reached the coupé, and he saw Ford Sheppard's hat roll out through the open door and hit the pavement. One look inside was enough to decide him. He sprinted back to his house, told his mother to call the police, and had returned to the coupé with his father and brother by the time Bert Westcott arrived. Perry knew better than to touch anything — he didn't even turn off the radio, which was still playing when I arrived — and he helped to hold off the crowd until Mr. Thorne got the firemen. So we had the best possible conditions under which to start work.'

Dickerson worried his moustache.

'You said he heard a 'dragging noise'. How did he describe it again?'

'Like a rat dragging an apple. Perry said that when he was in Sicily, the rats would come into his tent at night and steal food. He'd heard exactly the same sound and turned on his flashlight to spot a big rat dragging an apple across the dirt floor.'

'How far was he from the feed store when he heard the sound?'

'Not more than forty or forty-five feet.'

'A standard army tent is sixteen-by-sixteen feet; thus when he heard the rat in Sicily he could not have been more than six or seven feet from it. When he heard last night's sound, he was approximately seven times that distance from it. If we multiply the sound by seven times, we arrive at a pretty fair-sized rat.'

'I guess somebody was there, all right,' Boyle admitted. 'It's probably just as well that Perry investigated the coupé instead of the shadow.'

Dickerson nodded. Moving his coffee cup aside, he selected a photographic print that showed Ford Sheppard's body and the coupé's interior with faithful if grim detail. He studied it a moment, laid it carefully aside and picked up one that was of a thumbprint, greatly enlarged.

Boyle said, 'We didn't find many fingerprints. There were a few on the steering wheel, the door handle on the left side, the glove compartment door and on a bottle of scotch that was in the glove compartment. All of them were Sheppard's.'

'What about the right door handle?'

'There were no prints on it. Sheppard owned another car, a beach wagon, and he used it yesterday afternoon while the coupé was being washed and polished. The coupé wasn't touched until Shep entered it in his garage shortly after nine-thirty last evening. He'd had a visitor, Henry Heath, manager of the Kendall-Sudwich mill, and they were closeted in his study until about half-past eight, at which time Heath left. At about quarter of nine, Sheppard went up to his room, and the maids heard him taking a shower; when he came down again, he was freshly shaved and dressed. That's the last time they saw him alive.'

'Naturally he entered the coupé from the left side,' Dickerson mused. 'So we're more interested in the *right* door handle. The door on the right was the one that was open, and it was on the kerbside, was it not?'

'It was.'

'And yet there were no prints on either the inside or the outside handle of that door?'

'Correct. No prints.'

Dickerson rose to his feet. They'd had their meal in the kitchen, a large comfortable and square old room. Save for the installation of water pipes and the application of numberless coats of paint, the kitchen probably hadn't been changed in the seventy-five years since the house was built. Cooking was achieved on an enamelled coal range, an old-fashioned one equipped with a door that was hinged on the right side.

Dickerson inspected the coal range and reflectively chewed at his moustache. 'This ought to serve admirably,' he said. 'Anything in the process of baking?'

'Baking? No.'

'Good.' Dickerson opened the oven door to its full width. 'Here, in effect,' he said, 'we have the door of Ford Sheppard's Packard coupé. It stood open like this when first noticed by Perry Thompson — who, by the way, appears to have been a keenly observant person. Clearly, Ford Sheppard, a man who had just taken a bath, did not drive with an open door on a bitter March night; therefore it must have been opened after he reached his parking spot on Liberty Street. Although Sheppard wore no gloves, there were no prints found on the inner handle of this door. Therefore, clearly again, he did not open it.

'Now, let us stop a moment and consider what he was doing in that particular spot at ten o'clock at night. Before leaving his house, he had bathed, freshly shaved and dressed himself. Why? Obviously to keep an appointment. Why was his appointment set for that particular dark and secluded spot? The obvious answer is that the appointment must have been of a clandestine nature. If it had been otherwise, he would have parked in the well-lighted square so conveniently at hand. It was not a question of finding room; we understand that the sole automobile parked in the square was a station wagon occupied by Frederick Thorne.'

'Do you suppose,' Boyle asked slowly, 'that Sheppard might have been lured there? He was easy meat for a pretty face and a well-turned ankle.'

'I think not. We have the testimony of Perry Thomson that the Packard coupé was frequently parked there at night. This, of course, suggests a love triangle and a jealous husband tracking an erring wife to put a definite end, via a bullet, to the affair. But before we become too much involved in guesses, let us consider the evidence we have at hand. It is safe to assume that he had an appointment and was sitting in his car waiting for someone to arrive. And while he was waiting, that someone, or some other person, came along on the pavement and opened the door. Now, suppose you pick it up from there. What is immediately suggested to you?'

Boyle looked thoughtful. 'There weren't any prints on the outside handle. Therefore, whoever it was that came along and opened the door was wearing gloves. And the position of the body suggests that he was expecting someone — he was leaning over, only he didn't quite reach the latch before the person on the kerb opened the door.'

'Very good. Had he been unaware of the presence of a person outside, his body would have been found either in an erect position or slumped over the wheel. His head would have been turned to the right and, because of the interference of the top, would have received the bullet lower down. You have the coroner's report?'

Boyle found an envelope in his pocket, and from it withdrew a folded sheet. Spreading if before him he read:

'The bullet was a thirty-two calibre copper-jacketed ball from a centre-fire UMC cartridge. It entered the forehead directly over the line of the nose and about five-eighths of an inch above the eyebrows. Its course was downward and to the right, striking against the rear cranial bone at the bottom and leaving the skull above the top cervical vertebra. It was fired at a sufficiently close range, not more than twenty inches, to leave powder burns about the wound. Death,

if not instantaneous, was a matter of seconds thereafter. From all available evidence, it is the opinion of the undersigned that death occurred at a few seconds after ten p.m. Signed, Matthew Swale, M.D., coroner.'

Dickerson frowned. 'Did you find the cartridge?'

'No. We made a very thorough search under lights last night and in daylight this morning. No empty shell case was to be found. Swayle, who is a bit of a ballistics man, determined the make from unburned powder and priming found in the wound, and from the ball itself.'

'All right.'

Dickerson turned and, eyeing the open oven door, chewed laboriously at his moustache. And then he began to make magician-like passes at the kitchen stove. First he crossed his right arm over his left; shaking his dark, distinguished head, he crossed his left arm over his right.

'It just won't work,' Dickerson murmured.

Sergeant Boyle looked slightly alarmed.

'What won't work?'

'Notice this. Come over here beside me — that's it. You'd better kneel. There, that's fine.'

Sergeant Boyle got down on his knees beside Dickerson, who was also kneeling, and glanced at him in bewilderment.

'We are assuming that your kitchen range is the Packard coupé,' Dickerson explained. 'We will also assume that you have just walked up Liberty Street, on the pavement on the ledge side, and that your intention is to murder Ford Sheppard. We assume that you have come from *behind* the Packard, because had you come from the direction of the square he would have seen you, since you would have been silhouetted in the light. Am I making myself clear thus far?'

'Right.'

'Now, since you have come to commit murder, we will further assume that you carry a pistol, either openly in your hand or else concealed in your pocket ready for instant use. Now, with thumb and forefinger simulate a pistol, please.'

Dutifully, Sergeant Boyle stuck out the

thumb and forefinger of his right hand, giving inward thanks that Mrs. Boyle was somewhere else at the moment.

'Very good,' Dickerson said. 'Now I shall close the oven door. You have reached the side of the Packard and are about to open the door and shoot. Please do so.'

Sergeant Boyle swallowed. Reaching out with his left hand, he swung the oven open against himself, fumbled a bit in the process, crossed his right forefinger-extended hand over his left arm and, very solemnly, said: 'Bang!'

Dickerson chuckled. 'Awkward as the very devil, wasn't it?'

Sergeant Boyle scowled at the oven door. 'I got all fouled up with myself,' he said. 'Everything was in the way.'

'Exactly. Now suppose you try the same sequence, except that you will hold the imaginary pistol in your *left* instead of your right hand.'

Once again Sergeant Boyle dutifully obeyed, only this time it was the thumb and forefinger of the left hand that carried Dickerson's creative burden. The oven door opened easily; this time there was no fumbling to mar the smoothness of execution.

Boyle turned. 'The killer was left-handed,' he said simply.

Dickerson pulled himself to his feet with the aid of a kitchen chair and walked around a bit, dusting his knees by habit. The floor had been immaculately clean.

'From the coroner's report,' he said, 'and from the little experiment we have just conducted, it should be fairly safe to assume that the pistol was held in the killer's left hand. Later in the day we will verify this theory by examining Sheppard's coupé at the actual spot so that we may check the height of the kerb, the incline of the gutter and other factors. With reasonable luck, we may even be able thus to determine the killer's approximate height.

'But it's a little too early for us to assume definitely that the killer was left-handed. Many people are ambidextrous, and it must be remembered that the range was very close. At twenty inches, it would be hard for a man to miss with either hand.'

Boyle thought of something. 'What,' he asked, 'if instead of sneaking up Liberty Street, as we've figured, the killer had been sitting in the car, talking to Shep? Mightn't he or she have stepped to the kerb, turned and shot from the right hand?'

'I think not. The position of the body discounts such a possibility. So, let's sum up. Thus far we've smelled out a seven-times-sized rat dragging something. We have a reasonable idea of which way this rat came from and which way he went. We also have a fairly authentic notion that Sheppard was expecting someone, if not the actual killer. We know that our killer wore gloves and are reasonably sure that the pistol was fired from the left hand. And since you found no empty shell, we can assume that the weapon was a revolver type and not an automatic pistol. Now, have I missed anything?'

Sergeant Boyle stared at his stove dazedly. Missed anything? This quiet, unexcited man from Boston had been in Sudwich a little over two hours and he hadn't stepped out of the kitchen. Yet he'd taken the kitchen stove, a couple of photographs and the testimony of a few witnesses and out of them had constructed a picture that for fifteen hours had been eluding Boyle with all the evasiveness of a ghost.

'Gosh, I'm glad you're here,' was Boyle's fervent answer.

★   ★   ★

The public loves to be where it should not. And on this bright March afternoon, having discovered that the Cataract Hose Company was forming a solid phalanx across Liberty Street from Johnson's Feed Store to the ledge, the public migrated *en masse* to Mizzen Hill Road only to discover there an equally solid rearguard composed of the Alert Hook and Ladder Company. Frustrated, the public fell to wrangling within itself and dispersed to attempt other means of ingress to the suddenly important block length of Liberty Street. The more agile and adventurous were already assembled precariously near the brim of the ledge.

Those fortunate few who were residents saw from their front porch seats a mystifying and rather disappointing show.

They saw the Packard coupé standing in the exact spot at the kerb it had occupied the night before. They saw that the coupé's door was open and that a rather large and florid man, a black-moustached stranger dressed in a neat Oxford grey overcoat and a snap-brimmed grey felt hat, was standing by it. Immediately at hand was Jimmy Boyle, the state policeman whose father was a postman. Jimmy was holding a pole that for all the world looked like a surveyor's rod, and the stranger was bending down, moving a gadget on the pole and sighting through it into the open coupé.

Had they been close enough, the ones on the ledge would have heard the stranger say, 'Forty-four inches,' and would have heard Jimmy Boyle reply, after glancing at a card in his hand, 'Sixty-six to sixty-eight inches tall. Check.'

A lot of them *did* hear the stranger say, quite clearly, 'It holds up thus far.'

And then there was a deal of measuring

with a steel tape; a lot of bending and squinting and jotting down of figures.

As if they expected, with pencil and paper, to catch a murderer!

The stranger straightened up and said something to Jimmy Boyle, and Jimmy turned and beckoned. From the porch of house Number Twenty, young Perry Thompson came at a half-trot.

The stranger met Perry Thompson in front of the untenanted filling station. They talked a few minutes and Perry pointed, first to the coupé and then to the feed store. Then Perry returned to his house, walked up the drive and disappeared into the backyard.

A small boy suddenly lost his foothold and went howling down the face of the ledge. He didn't seem to be hurt much; the Cataract Hose Company converged slightly, but the lines held. He was rescued and speeded on his way by the gift of a nickel. The public loudly decided that the boy was Tommy Applegate, and there the matter rested.

In front of the filling station the stranger held aloft an inflated paper bag, and behind him Jimmy Boyle was glancing at a stop-watch. The stranger broke the bag with a satisfactory 'pop' and Perry Thompson presently appeared, walking down his drive.

Disappointing. Bert Westcott and Jimmy Boyle and Perry Thompson had been through the same rigmarole in the morning, only Bert Westcott had fired a blank cartridge into the air . . .

★　★　★

Dickerson stopped behind the feed store, turned to Perry Thompson and asked, 'You'd say it was about here?'

Perry Thompson nodded.

'And the dragging or shuffling sound you heard might have come from the shadow you saw?'

'I'm positive it did.'

Dickerson glanced down at the hard-packed gravelled drive, rutted from the traffic of many trips to the rear of the feed store and the bank. Abutting the driveway was a loading platform built of scarred planks whose cracks and crevices were laden with the leakage of countless meal and grain sacks. The platform was approximately twelve feet wide and six feet deep and extended not quite half the width of the building. Back in the angle of where the platform joined the clapboard wall, the gravel thinned out. There was a line of scattered dripstones, and beyond it earth containing the stalks of weeds and grain hugged the foundation line.

Dickerson said, 'He might have hidden there, in the angle of platform and wall, to avoid the light coming up the drive between this building and the bank next door.'

He moved, bending in search, seeking just what he knew not. Perry Thompson and the rest of them were forgotten now; here was the bloodhound in search of a scent. Almost at once, he saw how impossible a task he had set for himself. All along there, from the platform to the driveway between feed store and bank, wherever any earth lay exposed to form a matrix, it was hopelessly covered with a maze of tracks, marks and prints of every description.

Searching, he crossed the driveway and reached the rear of the bank building.

Here concrete steps descended into a well leading to the basement of the bank. Two ash-cans, one empty and the other nearly full, stood at the bottom of the steps. The floor of the stair well was of concrete, old and wrinkled with the cracks of many frosts.

Dickerson descended the steps and came up against a stout iron-barred door that was secured with an old Yale lock. Glancing around, he noted that the drive-way was just above the level of his eyes, and noted also what an excellent hiding-place the well would make. And then he was leaning forward, breathing fast with excitement.

On the inside of the iron handrail was a long smear of blood.

There wasn't much room for a man of his size, not with two ash-cans down there, but he managed to constrict and bend himself for a closer examination of the crumbling concrete floor. His eyes scanned the mossy crevices, covered the intervening space and travelled slowly up the door. His heart began to race when he discovered, in the angle between door and door jamb, approximately two and a half feet from the floor, another smear of blood.

Dickerson squatted there, puzzled, wondering why there should be blood in that particularly awkward place. There was none on the knob of the door and none, so far as he could see, anywhere else. Seeking an answer, his eyes searched slowly until they reached his feet, and there, not an inch from his toe, he found a strange mark. It was a triangular indentation in the moss; a hole five-eighths of an inch in width, an inch in depth and slightly tapering towards the base. It was located about eight inches from the heavily barred door and leaning towards that awkwardly placed smear on the jamb.

Too small, that mark, and not the proper shape for the print of a woman's high-heeled shoe.

Abruptly he got to his feet, climbed the steps and returned to the rear of the feed store, where Perry Thompson and Constable Westcott were standing and idly talking.

At his call, the constable turned and

came on dead-tired feet.

'Yessir?'

Dickerson said, 'I believe that when you arrived last night, you found a station wagon parked in front of the bank.'

The constable blinked sleepy eyes and nodded.

'Yessir. I came across the square from town hall in answer to the call from Perry Thompson's ma, and there was Mr. Thorne's station wagon and him in it.'

'Just what did Thorne say to you? What did he do?'

'Well, sir, when I came along by, he was just struggling to get out of his car — he's got a paralytic foot and he has trouble with the high kerbs, I guess — and I said to him, 'I just got a call from the Thompsons on Liberty Street. Did you hear a shot?' And he said, 'I heard something just about a minute ago.' And I asked him where had it come from and he thought it might be somewhere near the post office, but he wasn't sure. And then Perry came running out of the end of Liberty Street, so we went up and found the body in the Packard coupé.'

'You say that Thorne's a paralytic?' Dickerson asked thoughtfully. 'Does he carry a cane?'

'No, sir, never saw him with one. He gets around pretty good, flippety-flop fashion. Good enough to drive a car.'

'Then he didn't have a cane when you saw him last night?'

'No, sir.'

'Are you quite sure he was struggling to get *out* of his car? Might he have been trying, instead, to get back in it?'

'Well . . . ' Westcott blinked his sleepy eyes, 'I asked him what he was doing there and he said he'd stopped because he thought one of his lights was out. Then he heard the shot — I'd say he was getting *out* when I came up to him. Yes, sir.'

'Did you happen to notice if he was wearing gloves?'

'Gloves? No, sir, I didn't notice.'

'One more question. Did you see any indications of blood on his clothing, particularly on the cuffs or sleeves of his coat? There would have been enough of it to notice in the lights of the square.'

'Blood?' Westcott gasped. 'On Mr. Thorne? No, sir, he looked very clean to me. You wouldn't be thinking — '

From the driveway between bank and feed store arose a tumult of sound. A rushing, shouting clamour as if the stout lines had finally cracked and the public was having its way at last. Footsteps crunched on gravel, and a throng burst into view.

Jimmy Boyle was at the head of it, and he came directly to Dickerson. Jimmy's face was ghostly white and his blue eyes wide.

'It's — it's Tessie Morgan,' Boyle said in a strained voice. 'Over Kessler's grocery — one of the clerks went up to the stock-room for a case of tomatoes, and coming past her door he slipped in a big pool of blood. Tessie Morgan's dead. She was stabbed to death sometime last night!'

6

Swayle, the coroner, accepted Dickerson's presence as a matter of course. Swayle appeared to be entirely unperturbed by the fact of two murders almost at once in a town that hadn't even had a major burglary in two years. But, as Sergeant Boyle confided, Swayle made it a point never to be perturbed about anything because he had been the coroner's physician in New Haven before he 'retired' several years back to resume a general practice that police work had all but rendered extinct.

At the moment, Swayle seemed to be thoroughly enjoying himself. He and Frank, the husky and bearded photographer, were conversing merrily. Sergeant Boyle was at the telephone, making a preliminary report.

While waiting his turn, Dickerson frowned his way around the less congested area of the late Tessie Morgan's apartment and wondered what foible of her mind had caused her to put a bed in the living-room and a dining-room set in what ostensibly should have been a bedroom. In order for her to reach the dinky kitchenette, which was beyond the bath, she'd had to chase around her ridiculous canopied bed. And what did a single woman, living alone, want of a dining-room set, anyway? Why not living-room furniture?

He was not one given to forming hasty impressions, but a picture of the sort of woman Tessie Morgan had been was already formed in his mind.

It had started with the red-enamelled front door and had grown with the outlandish furniture, the purple velvet curtains and the ridiculous canopied bed. When you added to them the fact that Tessie Morgan had lived alone in the only apartment in a building that could be reached from two different streets, with plenty of opportunity offered for concealment — Dickerson chewed at his moustache and shook his head.

Was Tessie Morgan the woman for

whom Ford Sheppard had been waiting when he was killed? The rendezvous would have been convenient; it was just a few steps up the alley and past the filling station to where Sheppard's coupé was parked. But why then had he bothered to wait in his car? Why not come directly to the apartment? Or had he been waiting a signal from her and not wanted to be seen outside her door?

But no, that didn't jibe. Sheppard had been expecting someone to come along; he had been so sure that the someone had arrived that he'd leaned over to unlatch the door. That meant just one of two things: either it hadn't been Tessie that Sheppard was waiting for, or else it had been Tessie and for reasons of his own he did not care to visit her apartment. His reasons could have been many: fear of being compromised, or of being seen entering or leaving; the presence of a guest whom Tessie could not conveniently get rid of; or the fear of running into a jealous swain who might be checking Tessie Morgan's movements a little too closely for comfort.

And again, it might be that there wasn't even the remotest connection between the two slayings other than the long arm of coincidence. Ford Sheppard had been shot and Tessie Morgan had been stabbed. It was possible that the only parallel to be drawn between the two was that both had occurred in the same night.

It was Frank, the photographer, who discovered that the wiring was defective. He had been trying to rig a photo-flood for a time shot and had first blamed it on the bulb.

'Suppose it could be a fuse?' Frank grumbled. 'Or do you suppose the party who did the job might've pulled the main switch?'

Boyle had finished his telephone call at last. Squeezing himself through the restricted space near the door, he said: 'I noticed the box in the hall. I'll have a look.'

Dickerson had progressed to the window of the out-of-place dining-room and was examining the sill when his eyes happened to glance upward and notice that the catch fastener was broken cleanly off, and the part that remained was pulled nearly loose from its retaining screws. Some attempt to provide security had been made by wedging an ordinary yardstick between sash and frame, and he had not at first noticed it because the shade had been pulled partway down.

He had removed the yardstick and had leaned out of the raised window to inspect the fire escape when he saw marks in the sill and corresponding marks in the sash where a narrow jemmy or other similar instrument had been recently used. He withdrew, closing the window, and turned to find that the living-room was flooded with brilliant light.

Boyle had returned through the red-enamelled door to announce that the trouble was a blown fuse. 'I fixed it with a penny,' he said. 'Remind me to take it out before we leave. I don't want to set the building on fire.'

The bearded photographer changed plates and positions, performed a few minor contortions, and squeezed a rubber bulb. After he had held it, counting the seconds, he let go and said: 'Guess I'm finished, unless you've got something in there.'

Dickerson checked items in his mind. He'd rather expected to find some blood in the bathroom, with so much of it near the body in the other room, but there hadn't been any. And the kitchenette was just a made-over closet containing shelves and a dinky stove, an electrically operated two-burner affair. There was no sink; dishwashing must have had to be accomplished between the washbowl and the bathtub.

'There's a broken window catch in here,' Dickerson said. 'It was jemmied, and looks like a recent break. Boyle, you might dust it for prints, and when you're finished, it wouldn't hurt to have a shot with the sash raised to show both the broken catch and the marks in the sill.'

Boyle came in, and Frank transferred his equipment. Swayle sniffed and said, 'And to think he gets five bucks more for that.'

After a while, Boyle ruefully announced that there wasn't anything worth bothering with; Frank set up and made his picture, and then silently they came, irresistibly drawn by the thing in the other room.

Whatever beauty Tessie Morgan had possessed in life, in death she had found no dignity. Her prone, grotesquely twisted figure lay horribly still on the blood-drenched carpet between the foot of her canopied bed and the red-enamelled door. She had been dressed in a house-coat and feathered mules when the thing had happened to her. One of the mules had fallen off and lay near her bare foot at the edge of the carpet. On her left wrist a gaudy watch with broken crystal insisted the time was 9:33.

It was her face that affected them most of all. Her eyes were widely open with the insensible glaze of death. Spots of rouge stood out on her waxen cheeks, and her painted lips looked almost as if they might have been strips of carmined paper pasted on.

Dickerson stood above her, frowning down.

'From the position of the body, we see that she was standing when she received the wound,' he said, 'and it is quite evident that the thrust was delivered from a position in front of her; there are no marks on the head or throat to indicate that the slayer stood behind and held her while delivering the thrust.'

'Yep,' Swayle said. 'And now, if you're through, I'll have Boyle tell the boys to bring the basket. And a mop. I've got blood samples in case we need 'em. You want to see any more of her?'

'Not if you don't.'

'I'd like to've seen more of her when she was alive,' Swayle grunted, 'even if she did have a rep. Okay. Take her away.'

Two men brought in the basket and set it down. One of them, new at the job, kept his eyes averted and didn't seem to have much stomach for his work. Sergeant Boyle was pale, too, and his eyes were troubled. Suddenly he leaned over and pulled a blanket from the bed and covered the body with it.

'She wasn't such a bad kid,' Boyle said, as if his act had required an explanation. He then covered the bloodstains with sheets of kraft paper that had been obtained, at Dickerson's behest, from the store below. And the man with the mop, also at Dickerson's behest, confined his efforts to the hall.

Dickerson closed the red-enamelled door.

'Anything about that wound seem strange to you?' he asked of Swayle.

'Strange? Well, maybe. It was made with an extremely long knife. Through the heart, straight through between the ribs and into the lungs. A deep wound. Took strength and skill to deliver it.' Swayle scowled. 'Took some strength to pull it out, too. We've searched high and low, but there's no sign of the weapon.'

'Would you say the wound had been made with a knife, a stiletto or some type of bayonet?'

'Well, I don't know. Could've been any of 'em. It's a small, three-cornered wound. A bit too large for a stiletto, a bit too small for any bayonets I've ever seen. It was at least eight or nine inches long. Might've been a bayonet filed down, or it might've been a three-cornered file with the roughness ground off. I said 'knife' only to classify the general type of wound. I'd say it was done with a special weapon that might even have been made for the purpose.'

'Would you say that the depth of the wound might have been produced by a fall on the weapon?'

'You mean *hari-kiri*?' Swayle bridled, scenting an attempt to ring in a suicide theory. 'If that's so, where's the weapon?'

'I mean,' Dickerson patiently replied, 'the position of the body. When she fell, she fell forward; she was wearing mules, which afford insecure footing at best, and they tripped her and cast her headlong.'

Swayle sniffed. 'Possibly — but it doesn't alter the fact of murder, and that's the way I'm going to charge the jury.'

'It may not alter the fact of 'death at the hand of a person unknown',' Dickerson said gently, 'but it might conceivably alter the fact of the killer's strength. Aided by a headlong fall, the killer might be no stronger than, say, an ordinary woman. And right now I can think of a lot more reasons why a woman might want to kill

Tessie Morgan than I can for a man.'

'Well . . . ' Swayle looked annoyed. ' . . . it did take a strong person to pull it out. Unless it had a handle on it long enough for the use of both hands. And I've had enough experience — over thirty years of it — to know just how tough the human body is. Believe me, it takes a lot of strength, and skill, to deliver a death wound with a knife.'

Dickerson had no answer for that. A brief silence settled in the room, and Frank snapped the cover of his leather carry-all.

'Want me for anything more?' he asked.

Sergeant Boyle looked at Joe Dickerson, and Dickerson shook his head.

'Then I'll get to work on these,' Frank said. 'I'll have prints ready for you by six o'clock.'

There was a lot more room when Frank had gone. The man with the mop stuck his head in the door and asked, 'Now?'

Dickerson answered, 'Not yet,' and once again closed the door. Swayle asked if it would be all right for him to use the bathroom to wash his hands and Dickerson nodded in assent.

While the coroner was in the bathroom, Dickerson said to Boyle: 'There are a few points you'll want to check. When I first noticed the broken window catch, I thought that might have been the way the killer got in. But then I saw that a yardstick had been used for temporary repair, so obviously the window wasn't a factor last night. You might check with Kessler downstairs to see if Miss Morgan had recently reported a burglary, or Standish might have been called. And while you're on that angle, find out how many keys there were to this door. I don't believe we're going to have a whole lot of trouble with this.'

'Do you think it ties in with the other?' Boyle asked.

'I don't know. The difference in methods makes me wonder. You've been through her things?'

'Everything. Even under the galley stove. There wasn't hide nor hair of any papers or personal letters to be found. She had a portable typewriter, and there was the start of a business letter in it, but that's all.'

'Odd. Who did she work for?'

Sergeant Boyle's pleasant face darkened. 'That's the point. She was Henry Heath's secretary, at the mill, and Heath is the man who was at Sheppard's house an hour and a half before he was killed. And while I don't like to say it, frankly there was a lot of bad talk going around about Heath and Tessie.'

Swayle came in from the bathroom. He still looked slightly annoyed.

'I guess you won't need me for a while,' he said. 'I'll go down to the morgue — it's at Sudwich hospital.'

'Try to determine the time, will you, Doctor? The watch may have been broken before, or may have run down after.'

Swayle scowled. 'Offhand, I'd say the watch was right — I'll know better when I've checked the stomach contents.'

'On your way to the hospital,' Dickerson said, 'would you mind stopping at the rear of the bank? There's a stairwell leading down to the basement door, and on the door jamb, about two feet up from the cement bottom, you'll find a smear.

There are also smears on the inside of the handrail. In my opinion they are blood smears, and I'd like you to type them for comparison with your samples from Miss Morgan and Ford Sheppard.'

'Blood, in back of the bank?' Swayle scowled. 'It's probably paint. But I'll look, if it'll make you any happier.' Then Boyle suddenly recalled the penny in the fuse-box and followed the coroner into the hall.

The patient man with the mop asked hopefully, 'Now?' But once more the door was rudely closed in his face, and on the inside of it Dickerson had dropped to his knees to examine a three-cornered concave indentation, in area the size of a half-dollar, in the gleaming red-enamelled surface.

★ ★ ★

'I understand that Miss Morgan was in your employ,' Dickerson said when he had settled himself.

Henry Heath's eyes flicked about his office, and his hands worried a bronze paper-knife.

'Yes, she was,' he said nervously. 'Awful. Terrible thing. Can't get over it. Can hardly believe it.'

'Was she a good employee, punctual and all that?'

'Not particularly. She couldn't spell, and she had a terrible temper. But there was something about her you just couldn't help liking.' Henry Heath sighed. 'Poor kid!'

'Was she at work yesterday?'

'No. She telephoned at nine to say she was ill — I was out at the time, but one of the other women took the call.'

'Did she tell the woman what was wrong?'

'No.'

'Would you have any idea if there might be some person whom Miss Morgan would have reason to fear?'

'None in the world. We . . . ' The fat little man hesitated. 'We never had any confidences.'

'Then you wouldn't know who her friends were, her male friends in particular?'

'Oh, no — well, that is . . . ' Sweat

appeared above Henry Heath's collar. 'I believe she had been going fairly steadily with a young man named Ben Sutts, a local contract fisherman. Not too well educated, and with no background to speak of, but quite substantial.'

'Would you know if they had any plans to get married?'

'I'm afraid Mr. Sutts would have to answer that.'

Dickerson nodded. His face was masked with a sympathetic guileless little smile, but behind it he was wishing he could pin down just what it was about Henry Heath that didn't quite ring true. He was a lot more nervous than he was sad.

'I presume that you tried to get in touch with her when she failed to appear for work this morning?'

'Oh, yes. I telephoned several times. Of course, there was no answer. If only I had realized . . . ' Henry Heath sighed.

'How long had she been your secretary?'

'Seven or eight months.'

'And before that?'

'She worked here, in the mill.' At Dickerson's raised eyebrows, Heath added hastily, 'We have a personnel file, and when our last stenographer left to go to Washington for a government job, Mr. Kendall suggested that I see if one of our women might have a secretarial background. Tessie — Miss Morgan had taken a business course in high school, so Mr. Kendall decided to give her a trial.'

'Was he satisfied with her work?'

A faint frown of annoyance crossed Heath's perspiring face. 'I wouldn't exactly say he was satisfied. For some strange reason, he seemed to be very fond of her. I know she was the only person in the mill who dared to talk back to him, and she is one of the few people who have been permitted to see him since he has been confined. Mr. Kendall has been confined to his home since his son was reported missing in action in the South Pacific. He has a very bad heart condition.' Heath gave a long sigh, adding: 'Mr. Kendall is a most difficult man to understand sometimes. He also happens to be my father-in-law.'

Dickerson asked: 'Can you give me an

idea of any contacts, even minor ones, that Miss Morgan might have had beyond the personnel of the mill?'

'Well — I believe she sometimes posed for Fred Thorne, the well-known artist. He has a studio here.'

Dickerson sat straighter. He asked, 'How long ago did she pose for him?'

Heath's reply was lost in the unannounced arrival of a woman. Wearing a coat that was of good material, albeit unfashionable, and a prim hat, she came directly into the office, not stopping until she had reached Heath's desk.

Heath jumped to his feet. 'Prue! Didn't realize how late it was. Darn it, I keep reaching for my watch. What time is it, anyway?'

'It's nearly five, dear.'

'Sorry I kept you waiting. Oh, this is Mr. Dickerson. Mrs. Heath, my wife. Mr. Dickerson is with the state police.'

She inclined her head, smiling placidly, and Dickerson saw that she was rather small and plain and brown, with greyish skin and placid brown eyes. The whole effect of her was subdued, even depressing.

'How do you do,' she said. 'I suppose it's about Ford Sheppard. Of course Henry's told you that he was at Ford's last night. Right after supper, for about an hour.' She was looking at Dickerson but she said, 'You did tell him, didn't you, dear?'

Heath's face reddened. 'As a matter of fact, he hadn't asked me anything about Ford Sheppard,' he said bluntly.

'Oh, no? Well, really, there's nothing to hide. Ford had the mortgage on our house and it was due yesterday. My husband visited him in the morning and paid him the interest, but Ford asked him to return in the evening to see about recasting it.' This time her gentle voice was directed to Joe Dickerson, but her placid brown eyes remained on her husband.

Dickerson coughed. 'I'm quite sure, Mrs. Heath, we would have gotten around to it eventually. You see, I called because Miss Morgan had been your husband's secretary.'

Prudence Heath looked at Joe Dickerson now.

'*Had* been? Did you discharge her,

dear? I know she claimed she was too ill to work yesterday, but she wasn't too ill to have lunch with Ford Sheppard at the Iron Kettle.'

Henry Heath groaned. 'No. She was — she's dead.'

'Oh, the poor dear. An accident with her car, I suppose. She wasn't a very safe driver. Was anyone else hurt?'

That made Dickerson mad. She'd spoken of Tessie Morgan's death in much the same way she might have consoled one of her friends if some planted seeds had failed to come up. He said, 'Miss Morgan was murdered in her apartment last night at some time shortly before ten o'clock.'

Prudence Heath said, 'Oh,' in a faint voice, and Dickerson, accustomed as he was to gauging reactions, couldn't decide whether she was shocked or relieved.

★   ★   ★

Walking back to Sudwich Square, Dickerson decided he couldn't make out Mrs. Heath. Was she very stupid or extremely smart? Certainly, she was extraordinary. Her mannerism of looking at one person and talking to another was decidedly annoying. And he wondered if, after waiting somewhere for her husband to meet her and then walking through the town, she expected him to believe she'd had no knowledge of Tessie Morgan's murder. Had she a definite purpose in blurting out the information that her husband had visited Ford Sheppard on the night that Sheppard was killed? Sheppard had been killed at ten o'clock, and Heath might have been able to establish a solid alibi for that hour. But could he account for his time a half-hour earlier, when Tessie Morgan was meeting violent death 'at the hands of a person or persons unknown'?

And why had she volunteered the information that Miss Morgan, although claiming to be too sick to work, had apparently been well enough to have lunch with Ford Sheppard?

Dickerson frowned and chewed at his moustache with annoyance. Regardless of how much 'bad talk' there might have been about Heath and his secretary, it was ridiculous to think of the fat, soft little man as a murderer. A philanderer, perhaps, fearing to be caught and mercilessly exposed by the chain of circumstance. At each of Dickerson's attempts to establish more than a purely business relationship between Heath and his secretary, the man had become increasingly nervous, betraying himself with most evident relief when the subject switched to safer ground.

This was interesting, but it only annoyed Dickerson. He had been sent to Sudwich for the express purpose of working on the Sheppard case. The commissioner would be expecting his report on that, no matter if half the town of Sudwich was murdered. Unless a direct connection with the Sheppard affair could be established, the commissioner wouldn't be interested.

Was there a connection? Was it logical that two murders in which two different weapons were used would be committed by the same person within a half hour of each other? It would be logical if the shooting had occurred *first;* since both slayings had occurred within sound of each other, the killer might well have sought to escape immediate detection and capture by resorting to the soundless knife, for within a half-hour of the murder of Ford Sheppard there had been so many people milling in and about the general area that a revolver shot would have brought a frenzied mob on the slayer's heels so swiftly that flight would have been impossible.

But in this strange affair the knife, or whatever it was, had apparently been used first. And as Swayle had pointed out, the killer had to be pretty sure of himself; the human body is tough, and by far more victims of carving affrays recover than are ever sent to the morgue. Was Tessie Morgan's death an accident? Miss Morgan had fallen forward, and the end of the weapon had struck her red-enamelled door to drive the point even more deeply home.

Thus, Dickerson could visualize, a defence attorney would argue. But there was one irreparable flaw in that argument: if the death had in truth been accidental, *why had the weapon been removed?* Unthinking fear would have prompted an accidental slayer to immediate flight, with weapon and all else forgotten.

No, the death of Tessie Morgan had been carefully planned and coolly executed for a definite purpose, yet to be determined. If chance was present anywhere in it, that chance might rest in the method; for to Dickerson's logical brain, schooled in the ways of killers, it was entirely possible that the slayer might have conceived a plan only to abandon it instantly when a simpler and apparently safer method by chance presented itself.

If this should prove to be the case, then the difference in method between the two slayings would have no bearing; indeed, that difference could have been premeditated by a shrewd murderer. It could have been carefully planned, just as, for instance, the trick of firing the pistol from the left hand must have been planned.

What, then, would be the purpose or motive? Was it revenge? Was there some thwarted individual in the background whose ego demanded that the luscious playgirl and the handsome playboy must die? Did Tessie Morgan and Ford Sheppard share some secret, perhaps unknown to each other, that threatened the security or happiness or perhaps even the life itself of another?

Dickerson didn't know, and he was far too sensible to hazard a guess before assembling all the facts. Of one thing only was he certain: while the removal of both Tessie Morgan and Ford Sheppard might conceivably have been to the advantage of either Heath or his wife Prudence, it was the internationally famous Frederick Thorne who, at the moment, had the most explaining to do.

* * *

Dickerson had progressed as far as the square when he saw Sergeant Boyle bounding down the steps of the Town Hall, followed by a somewhat haggard-looking Constable Westcott.

'We've had a break,' Boyle said excitedly. 'The people in Kessler's heard a terrific argument yesterday morning between Tessie Morgan and Ben Sutts. It progressed to the point where several blows, plainly audible to the people in the store, were either struck or exchanged. I haven't been able to contact Sutts as yet; he's out on his boat and it isn't due in to dock until about seven. And here's another item; you recall that broken window catch?'

'I do.'

'The post-office janitor swears that he saw Sutts climbing her fire escape at a little before nine o'clock the night before last. He had just come out from checking the boiler in the post-office building, and there's an unobstructed view of the back of Kessler's. The lights from the square shine through there, and the janitor says he couldn't possibly have been mistaken.'

'Hm. This argument . . . any idea of what it was about?'

'None, except that Kessler said it was a honey. He had a couple of customers in the store at the time — Ford Sheppard's maid and housekeeper — and he was greatly embarrassed.'

'Ford Sheppard's?'

'Yes. Quite a coincidence, isn't it?'

Dickerson thought that there were beginning to be just too many coincidences. He said: 'When you see Swayle, have him examine Sheppard's hands and clothing for any blood spots that might not be his own. Tell Swayle to dig under the fingernails and pare into the cuticle. And while you're at it, see if he's got an analysis of the blood stains I told him about.'

Boyle grinned. 'Those are suggestions, I suppose?'

'They are.' Dickerson smiled. 'And after you've done all that, I suggest you contact someone in the bank who can give you a list of the persons who would possess keys to the cellar door, and find out if the front door can be opened from the inside without the use of a key. Do it unobtrusively if possible. I don't want to set them on their ears.'

'That'll be a cinch. My sister Margaret works in the savings department.'

'Good. And when you've covered that, I suggest you catch a couple of hours' sleep. It's entirely possible that we may have a lot to do tonight.'

'Sleep,' Bert Westcott said hoarsely. 'Where did I hear that word before? Brother, if somebody pushed me now, I wouldn't get up for a month.'

'I wish we had another man,' Dickerson said. 'I've got one, but I'm holding him in Boston to cover any angles that may crop up there. Do you know at what time the night operator goes on in the local telephone exchange?'

'She goes on at eight.'

'Good. That'll give me time to eat supper, try to figure out some sort of a report for the commissioner, and find a place to stay.'

'A place to stay? What's wrong with my place?' Boyle demanded. Grabbing Dickerson by the arm, he started him along the street. 'Your grip is in the spare room already, and if you aren't at the table by six, Mrs. Boyle will be sore because she's got something special. And incidentally, she thought that maybe Mrs. Dickerson might have wanted to know where you were and that you'd have forgotten to tell her, so she called her up. And don't you let Mrs. Boyle know that I told you where she got the recipe, or she'll crown me!'

★　★　★

Dickerson, having been properly 'surprised' and appreciative when Mrs. Boyle set his favourite Spanish omelet before him, didn't need to feign enjoyment. It was done to a perfection that would have made the Copley Plaza's head chef himself silent with envy.

Over that good woman's strong objections, Mrs. Boyle found herself assisted with the dishes. Dickerson wiped and the two small Boyles formed an efficient brigade.

And so it was that the kitchen was as clean and shining as a new pin and Dickerson was seated at the enamel-topped table, laboriously chewing his moustache and making pencilled notes in a small and dog-eared memo book when Sergeant Boyle returned.

The sergeant went straight to the oven, found the two egg sandwiches and the coffee that had been set aside for him and, returning, plunged directly into the business of eating and reporting.

'Sutts brought his boat in a little earlier than usual tonight,' Boyle said, 'because storm warnings have been posted, so I was able to see him right after I left you. He has an amazing story, and one of the best alibis I've ever run up against. I'm going to repeat the story first, and then I'll give you the alibi and you can draw your own conclusions.

'On Wednesday night, the night before Tessie Morgan was killed, Sutts had a date with her. Early Wednesday morning, before going out in his boat, Sutts had called her at the mill and arranged to meet her at seven p.m. to take her to the local movies. The picture was one she had previously expressed a desire to see, and she seemed entirely in accord with the arrangement.

'According to Sutts, and his statement is substantiated by people around the dock, he had four boats out that day and they had meagre luck until along towards evening when they ran into a school of pollack near William's reef, and then all hands were extremely busy. Sutts, however, remembered his date, and promptly at half-past five came alongside the smallest boat, boarded her and ordered the helmsman, Manuel Zella, to head for the dock. There was an argument with the other two crew members on this score because they fish on shares and stood to lose money. Sutts settled it, however, by offering them a bonus of ten dollars each and guaranteeing them an equal share in the entire haul, and so they were satisfied.

'The arrangement he had made had been to pick up Tessie at her apartment, and so he was there, freshly shaved and dressed in his best suit, at the stroke of seven. She, however, was not at home, so he went back to his car to wait. Wednesday night was very cold and Sutt's car was not equipped with a heater. There is a tavern directly across the street from the Kessler store, and so Sutts repaired there to keep warm and at the same time keep watch. Although he did not himself indulge, he justified his presence by purchasing a round of drinks for the customers, and so the proprietor was content to permit him to occupy a stool at the end of the bar. A number of acquaintances approached him and talked to him on various subjects, mostly political, but he managed to keep an eye on the entrance to the alley alongside Kessler's store, and in the progress of an hour-and-a-half's time Tessie Morgan did not appear.

'During that period, a change occurred in the atmosphere of the tavern. His acquaintances gave up trying to make conversation with him, and it became evident to all concerned that he had been given the proverbial stand-up.

'By now,' Boyle continued, 'Sutts was mad, and he was getting madder by the minute. In addition to mental distress, he had thus far expended better than thirty dollars to be able to keep his end of the bargain. So at nine o'clock he crossed the street and once again mounted the stairs. The results were negative as before, and since he did not possess a key, he secured a heavy screwdriver from his car, and going to the rear of the building climbed the fire escape, forced the window and let himself in. This part of his story checks exactly with the report of the post-office janitor.'

Boyle got up, walked to the stove and poured himself another cup of coffee before resuming his narrative. 'Sutts says that he crossed through the dining-room, entered the combination living-room and bedroom, and turned on the light and sat down to wait. And while he waited, he reflected that this was not the first time Tessie had done this to him. He had bought her a car, had helped her with the payments on her portable typewriter, and had in many other ways rendered her assistance.

'Sutts insisted to me that he had always acted the part of a gentleman, and that their relationship had progressed no further than an occasional good-night kiss or hand-holding in the movies. Sutts said that he respected the fact that Tessie was engaged to Bill Stanczyk, a Marine who is missing in action along with another local boy, Cotton Kendall, in the South Pacific. But as soon as the matter of Stanczyk's status was satisfactorily cleared up, he had intended to ask Tessie to be his wife.

'But after he had waited until nearly midnight, had made a few cautious telephone calls to the mill and to other places where Tessie might legitimately be found and had done a lot of thinking, he finally realized that he was being played for a sucker. And so, at midnight, Tessie not having returned, he went home, sat in his kitchen and drank a bottle of beer.

'It was here that he was found by Manuel Zella. Manuel had just come from the Well-House Tavern, a roadhouse about two miles out of town, and there he had seen Tessie in the company of a sailor. According to Manuel's report, Tessie had been quite drunk and very affectionate.

'On hearing this, Sutts says that he was at first of a mind to get in his car and go punch the sailor in the nose. And then he remembered he was a candidate for selectman, and such an act might not meet the approval of the voters, so he desisted. He did, however, decide to visit Tessie the following morning and to tell her off and part company with her forever.

'And this he did, using the fire escape as on the previous night. Although it was eight o'clock and nearly time for her to be at work, he found her still in bed. He did not awaken her and merely sat, thinking over his grievances, until nine when her telephone rang and the noise roused her. Then, he said, the argument began and ended when he spanked her. With a few appropriate remarks, he left the apartment at approximately half-past nine; and that, he claims, was the last time he ever saw or intended to see her.'

Boyle paused and finished his coffee. 'Remembering the absence of a diary or any personal correspondence, I expressly asked him if he had removed any letters. His reply was no, that he wasn't the writing kind, and anyway why would he write her since they both lived in the same town? I pointed out to him that he was liable on a charge of breaking and entering, and he shrugged and said he would face it if necessary. I asked him if he had any idea as to who might have killed either Tessie or Ford Sheppard and he said he had none. And that,' Boyle concluded, 'was his story.'

Glancing up from his pencilled hieroglyphics, Dickerson said, 'All this took place on Wednesday night and Thursday morning, on which day Miss Morgan was killed. Plenty of motive there, all right, especially if it can be shown that Ford Sheppard was beginning to make time with her. I'm afraid that alibi you spoke of will have to be awfully good.'

'Good?' Boyle smiled sadly. 'It's perfect. Sutts was out all day on his boat, which came in to dock at a little after seven p.m. According to medical evidence and the broken watch, Tessie was killed between nine and ten p.m. And from the hour of eight until after ten, Ben Sutts was on the platform at the Polish-American Club, attending a political rally. Somewhere during that time he made a speech, and there are between thirty and forty witnesses who won't be apt to forget him because it took him an hour to get out a couple of hundred words.'

7

The Sudwich telephone exchange was housed in a converted dwelling near the railroad station, and as Dickerson entered and crossed through the now-empty business office, the hands of a large electric clock pointed to fifteen minutes past eight.

Beyond a railed-in enclosure, a pebbled-glass door bore the warning 'No Admittance'. But sound and light both issued from behind it, and unabashed, Dickerson passed through.

Leaning over the counter, he grinned and said, 'Hello, Toots.'

The woman at the switchboard swung around, lifting the headphone from her ear. She attempted a stern look, but her eyes didn't give her much help. 'Aren't you kind of old to be running around saying things like that?'

'A man is as old as his memories,' Dickerson said gallantly, 'and many's the day since I've set eyes on a colleen as pretty as you.'

She laughed. 'What do you want, anyway?'

'Were you on the board last night?'

'Sure, and I'll be gracin' it again tomorrow night and every night until next Wednesday. So if it's a date you're wanting, write your name and address on the pad and I'll put it in the hat along with the rest of 'em.'

Dickerson grinned. 'That's not why I'm here. I, Toots, am a state cop.'

'My name isn't Toots, it's Jennie.' She looked him over thoughtfully, and nodded. 'So you're the one Jimmy Boyle called about. Haven't seen you around here before. You must be from Hartford.'

He didn't argue the point. 'I'm interested,' he said, 'in any calls Ford Sheppard might have made or received at about this time last night, or other nights during the week.'

For a moment she was busy with the switchboard, and her fingers flew with plugs and lines. Then, 'I don't keep a record of individual calls, you know.'

'Sure, but you don't have so many this time of night that you couldn't remember a few. Your mind automatically registers and groups calls; you get accustomed to certain voices; you get to know certain people pretty well without ever seeing them.'

'Say, you're kind of shrewd, aren't you?' Jennie said, wrinkling her pert nose. 'It's against company policy. You'll have to get an order from the supervisor.'

'I've already seen the supervisor. I've got it here.'

The woman laughed. 'All right. I came on the board at eight last night. I guess maybe I'd been on about an hour when Ford Sheppard called the Kendalls' number.'

Dickerson made a doodle on the pad. 'The Kendalls. You wouldn't have happened to hear, now, who it was he asked to speak to at the Kendall house?'

'I wouldn't have heard,' she said, and there was a trace of hardness in her voice. 'But whoever it was he wanted must not have been there because he hung up right away.'

And then three lights winked at once and she was busy for a time. When she was finished, she turned about and asked, 'Are you still here?'

'Yep. Tell me, were there many such

calls between the Sheppard and Kendall houses?'

'Many? No. Not during my hours. Not enough to notice.'

'Were there any other calls to or from Sheppard's house while you were on last night?'

'There were plenty of them after eleven o'clock, believe me.'

Dickerson frowned. 'This call he made. Could it have been to a woman?'

'It could have been,' she said, and her voice was reluctant.

Dickerson made more doodles. 'Who would I have to see, now, to ask about calls during the day?'

'The supervisor. We have four women on during the day. I don't wish you any hard luck, but I've been on day work and I know how hard it is to remember all the calls that come through.'

'To get back to this call Sheppard made to the Kendall house: would you have heard, some other night perhaps, a similar call? Would he have been making a date, maybe?'

'See here, mister.' The woman suddenly

looked him straight in the eye. 'I know that you've been poking around town and asking questions, and you've probably run into some gossip. Marion Kendall is the wife of Cotton Kendall, and he's been missing in the South Pacific for the past five months. It just happens that I've got a brother who's a marine, and he's out there too. And I went to school with Bill Stanczyk; he was Cotton Kendall's gunner and crashed in the same plane with him. I know what Marion Kendall has been going through. She's a real lady, and that's why you'll hear a lot of little people trying to run her down. But I don't want you to get any wrong ideas about her from me.'

Dickerson did some rapid thinking. 'Did Cotton Kendall happen to know Frederick Thorne, the artist?'

'Actually, they were close friends. As long as I can remember, before Cotton went away they were as close as any two people ever were. It's sort of a local legend that Cotton was the one who encouraged Mr. Thorne in his painting — Oh, this dratted board! Excuse me!'

When she finished and faced about, Dickerson said, 'Can you recall if Frederick Thorne put through or received any messages last night?'

'Oh, yes. That's an easy one! He has an unlisted phone, and it's quite a nuisance when he gets an out of town call. Sarah Barnes, the woman I relieved, said that some doctor in Boston had been trying to get him all afternoon, and she'd finally been able to put the call through at half-past seven, and it was a long one. Then, at shortly after nine, just after the New York Express stopped, there was a call for him from the pay telephone at the station; it was a horrible voice, one I'd never heard before. And a little after that, Mr. Thorne called the Kendall house first, and then he called the Dunes Club. There weren't any others after that.'

Dickerson was no longer doodling. His dog-eared memo book was out and he was putting down meticulous hieroglyphs in it.

'Um, now about Tessie Morgan. Would you happen to remember any calls for her?'

'There weren't any after I came on. You might check with the other women. She didn't get many. When she did, they were usually from Ben Sutts or . . . ' Jennie hesitated.

'Or some other man,' Dickerson supplied. 'Tell me, wasn't Tessie supposed to be engaged to Bill Stanczyk?'

Jennie blushed a bit. 'I guess you might call it that,' she admitted. 'They were going pretty steady, and he was awfully jealous . . . You know, life is a strange thing,' she said, reflecting. 'There was Cotton Kendall, a rich man's son, and Bill Stanczyk, a poor boy. Both of them were born in Sudwich and lived here most of their lives, but they had to go halfway around the world to meet each other. And then they were shot down.' She sighed and added, 'I guess you'd almost call it fate. Sort of like an appointment with destiny.'

★ ★ ★

The tired-looking woman behind the counter in the telegraph office was just putting on her hat and taking a last glance around when Dickerson came in. She favoured him with a hostile glare, reached for the pull-cord of the sole remaining light and said quite firmly, 'Sorry, but we're closed.'

Dickerson was forced to display the credentials Sergeant Boyle had furnished him with, but he softened the blow. 'I won't detain you more than a minute. Tell me, how do you deliver your casualty messages from the War and Navy Departments?'

'The company is very strict about that,' the woman said. 'We have a lot of regulations set up for us. We try to deliver the message directly to the person concerned; if that person is ill or, as in some cases, expecting a baby, we get the co-operation of the physician. We follow the same procedure as all our larger offices.'

'And in case of good news? That is, if a person classified as Missing in Action had been found?'

'The same way if possible. Telegrams are delivered directly by our boys. If the person addressed is away, we make every effort to contact them through our other offices.'

Dickerson said, 'Can you recall receiving the telegrams about Kendall and

Stanczyk being missing in action?'

'No. That was some time ago, I believe. I've only been here a month. Mr. Caton was the manager then. He's been drafted — I suppose I could check the files, if you insist.'

'That won't be necessary. Would you know if a second telegram had come about either of the boys, a notification that he'd been found?'

'Cotton Kendall or Bill Stanczyk found? No. Not since I've been here. I'm certain there hasn't been such a message. The news would be all over town if there had been. I can check the files, but it'll take some time.'

'Tomorrow will do,' Dickerson said. 'You can reach me at the Boyle residence. And I'll have to ask you to handle the matter yourself. While you may trust your clerks, the presence or absence of such a telegram may have a direct bearing upon one or both of the murders which were committed here last night. A leak might prove most embarrassing to our investigation, and I must therefore ask you to confide in no one.'

The woman digested that. Then: 'My clerks?' she gasped. 'Say, where do you think you are, in New Haven or someplace? In this town it's a wonder I don't have to deliver the messages too!'

★   ★   ★

Dickerson sat in the pay-booth in Sanford's Drug Store and hoped that Jennie, who was mighty sharp, hadn't recognized his voice. And as he waited for the commissioner to come on, the thought occurred to him that, although Tessie Morgan had possessed an automobile, for some reason it hadn't seemed to be in evidence. They hadn't found the key for it; in fact they hadn't found any keys amongst Miss Morgan's effects. Could it be that Ben Sutts had —

★   ★   ★

'Commissioner?'

A 'YES!' exploded in his ear. He gave a preliminary report that contained just enough hint of progress to keep the commissioner's hairy paws from ripping the telephone from its moorings. When Dickerson admitted, with fingers crossed, that there were practically no clues, and reminded him about the promise of co-operation and asked for it in the form of a couple of extra men, the commissioner's 'NO!' nearly split the receiver.

Dickerson grinned, held the circuit open and requested the Boston operator to switch him to Doctor Julian Martens.

Martens was at home. The surgeon's quick brain caught Dickerson's guardedness and responded in kind.

'The patient? Er — yes. I called the artist a short while ago, and while I was unsuccessful in getting further information, he has promised to communicate with me. I tried several times to get in touch with you today before I was finally informed that you were in Sudwich. Has your — er — trip anything to do in connection with the patient?'

'It may, and again it may not. Would it be possible for you to come here tomorrow to see the artist about a pastel portrait?'

'Let me see . . . Perhaps it could be

arranged. Are there any instructions in regard to the patient?'

'No. A Mr. Connelly will call in the morning. The commissioner is instructing him to co-operate with your 'department'.'

'Excellent! Where can I reach you at, say, eight in the morning?'

Dickerson gave him the telephone number of the Boyle house, and as he hung up he wondered just how much of the conversation had made sense to Jennie if she had been curious enough to listen in.

★   ★   ★

It was past midnight when Sergeant Boyle awoke with a start and sat up, fully clothed except for his shoes, to discover Dickerson sitting beside him on the bed. Dickerson was holding a tapered triangular stick in his hands. The stick appeared to be some sort of a straight cane, recently whittled out of a piece of ordinary white pine.

Sergeant Boyle yawned and blinked his eyes. 'Where've you been, and what's that you've got there?' he asked.

'Down at the station, watching the trains. A cane,' Dickerson answered in succinct sequence. 'Any time you're ready, we'll start on the next leg of our journey.'

Boyle said, 'Give me a minute to wake up.' He swung his stockinged feet from the bed and moved headed to the bathroom. When he returned, his wet hair was neatly combed and drops of water were running down his neck. He looked at Dickerson.

'You were saying?'

'At nine-thirty I picked up Swayle's report. Sheppard had type three blood, while Miss Morgan's was type one. The smears on the handrail and the door jamb in the rear of the bank were also type one, but there was no type one blood to be found anywhere on Ford Sheppard.'

'Which means?'

Dickerson shrugged. 'We now know that Sheppard did not kill Miss Morgan. Also, we have narrowed the distance between the killing of Miss Morgan and the killing of Ford Sheppard to slightly less than fifty yards. Swayle confirms the broken watch; we can put Miss Morgan's death as between nine-fifteen and nine-forty p.m. The presence of the smears at the rear of the bank establishes the presence of Miss Morgan's killer there at some time between nine-thirty and ten, when Sheppard was killed. So I think it no longer necessary to question the theory that both slayings were committed by the same person.'

'It fits,' Boyle admitted, thinking. He reached in the pocket of his shirt to produce an index card. 'I have the list you asked for. These are the people who are checked out with keys to the basement.' He grinned. 'And I also got a key from Ben Sprague, the janitor. I figured you'd want it.'

'Good work!' Dickerson exulted. Accepting the list, he scanned it and read slowly: 'Calvin Cartwright, president; Aldus Tumulty, vice-president; Max Kessler, Edward Kendall, Eugene Cotton Kendall and Clarence Marie, directors; Harold Finch, cashier and Ben Sprague, janitor.' Dickerson looked up, frowning. 'Wonder why they didn't pick up Cotton Kendall's key when he left to go in service?'

222

'Couldn't say. It does seem a bit careless. Incidentally, you asked if it was possible to open the front door from the inside without a key. It is.'

'Then anyone who possessed a key to the cellar door had practically the run of the bank?'

'Not exactly. The vault is quite modern, equipped with a time lock, and the book-keeping and accounting department is located in a fire-proof room which is kept locked during the hours in which the bank is closed, and I understand Finch is the only person who has a key to that room. So actually a person having a key to the cellar door would only have access to the portion which is normally open to the public during banking hours. That includes the basement, because the toilets are located down there.'

Dickerson chewed thoughtfully at his moustache. 'Do you have anyone covering that area tonight?'

'Yes. The selectmen have put on Perry Thompson as an extra constable. They asked me to suggest someone who has a good head on his shoulders.'

Dickerson chuckled. 'Then maybe Perry won't mind turning his back while we break into the bank.'

★ ★ ★

The beam from the powerful torch in Boyle's hand cut a bright hole in the darkness behind Johnson's feed store, licked the scarred planking of the loading platform, swung beyond to touch Liberty Street and its flanking ledge, and returned to dwell briefly on the rear of the bank.

'Notice the stairwell leading to the basement of the bank,' Dickerson said in a low tone. 'A person hidden down there would have been perfectly placed to watch all traffic coming up Liberty Street from the direction of Mizzen Hill Road. Thus the slayer could have waited until Ford Sheppard's Packard was spotted as it passed by the filling station and coasted to its parking spot. You will also notice that the alley alongside the bank affords a fairly good view of the square. Thus whoever it was hidden down there had only to wait until Sheppard's car appeared, glance up the alley to make sure that no one was approaching Liberty Street from the square, and then proceed with comparative safety. The only point of possible danger which could not be covered from that place would be the Post Road hill, but the high ledge would afford concealment from motorists, and at ten o'clock at night there would be little to fear from pedestrians.'

A form materialized suddenly in the darkness and a flashlight picked them out. 'Oh, it's you. Good evening, sir. Good evening, Sergeant.' And Perry Thompson came up.

Dickerson said, 'Glad to see you on the job. Are you keeping an eye on Miss Morgan's apartment?'

'Yes, sir. I've been up there several times, but so far nothing has stirred. I've made a couple of discoveries, though.' Perry Thompson hesitated.

'What have you discovered?'

'Well . . . Probably you've noticed it too, but you can't see any of the area between Kessler's and the post office from here because of the way Kessler's stockroom makes an ell at the back of the building. And while you can see through into the square between the post office and the bank from the dining-room window in Miss Morgan's apartment, you can't see Dock Street because there's a jog in the wall there.'

Dickerson nodded. 'I see. What does it suggest to you?'

Perry Thompson leaned forward eagerly. 'It means that the person who killed Miss Morgan wouldn't have risked getting into her apartment by the fire escape because he could have been seen by anyone passing in the square. So he must have gone up the stairs from the alley and got in by her front door, which means he either had a key and let himself in, or she knew who he was and let him in. And here's another thing too. Tessie used to park her Ford coupé in back of the post office, and the janitor is positive it was there Thursday night, but it wasn't there Friday morning and it isn't there now.'

Boyle nudged Dickerson. 'What did I tell you about him having a head on his shoulders?'

Dickerson said, 'Good work, Perry.

We'll check that car angle. Maybe Ben Sutts decided to take it, since he was paying for it. You might make some inquiries of the janitor, and also of the tavern proprietor.'

Thompson grinned. 'Yes, sir. I'll see what can be done.'

When Perry had gone, Dickerson motioned to Boyle to have the torch in readiness, and together they proceeded to the stair-well leading to the bank's basement. Boyle turned the light down and they saw that the ash-cans had been removed.

They reached the foot of the stairs, and Sergeant Boyle was forced to remain standing on the lower step while Dickerson knelt down on the crumbling concrete floor. And now, for the first time, Boyle began to realize just what Dickerson's crudely whittled cane was for.

'Notice,' Dickerson whispered. With the small end of the cane he pointed to a triangular indentation in a mossy crevice, still visible although it had been considerably scuffed since its discovery in the afternoon. And then Dickerson fitted the smaller tapered end into the hole and permitted the cane to lean until its head rested in the angle between door and jamb.

'Now if you will flash your light at the head of the cane, you will see where some of the blood smear still remains on the door jamb. The rest of it was removed by Doctor Swayle for his analysis. I reconstructed this cane from the indentation in the moss, estimating the length from the distance between indentation and smear, and securing the shape of the head from a mark taken from the inside of the red-enamelled door in Miss Morgan's apartment. And the analysis has showed us that the blood of this smear and the smears on the handrail are of the same type as Miss Morgan's blood.'

'Do you mean to say Tessie was killed with an ordinary cane?' Boyle asked incredulously.

'No, not an ordinary cane. In years gone by, when tall ships were lying at Sudwich wharf, it was both fashionable and practical for the gentlemen who did business to protect themselves by carrying sword-canes. I've no doubt that a search of Sudwich attics would bring to light many such an old weapon. But this one appears to have been of a distinctive shape, and it is possible that we shall have luck enough to trace its origin. Let's get inside before the town gets an idea that we're trying to rob the bank.'

Janitor Sprague's key admitted them to the warmth of the basement, and Boyle's torch picked out objects until it came to rest on the light switch. Dickerson flicked the switch on, and as the objects in the cellar became defined, his eyes sought the windows, saw that there were only two of them located in the rear and none in the side walls, and saw that these windows were tightly covered by heavy shutters.

Dickerson opened the door and stepped outside, closing it for a moment, and then came in again. His eyes were bright with satisfaction. 'Thought so,' he said. 'As I recalled, the blackout regulations along this stretch of the coast were particularly severe. Not a chink of light escapes those windows or this door. You realize what that means?'

'It means,' Boyle answered slowly, 'that the killer could have been in here, cleaning himself up, while we were tramping around right outside the door — I even came down into that darned stairwell myself.'

'Right. All we've got to do now is to establish the killer's presence inside this door, and we'll be on a definite trail.'

They separated and began a search that did not end until they had covered the entire basement, had mounted the stairs and crossed through the public space of the banking room itself to reach and open the front door, and had returned again to the cellar. And there they looked at each other with blank disappointment.

'Well, that's that,' Dickerson said. 'There isn't any evidence that our friend ever passed beyond this basement door. Either he cleaned himself up without leaving a trace, or he never entered.'

'He was wearing gloves,' Boyle suggested. 'Might he have burned them in the furnace?'

'It's possible. Unfortunately, the ashes have been removed. You might make it a point tomorrow to find out from the janitor where that particular batch of ashes was dumped. If they were snap-on gloves, some bits of twisted and melted metal might remain: if they were gauntlets, I doubt if we'd ever be able to distinguish such a small quantity of leather ash from coal ash, and if they were fabric gauntlets we'd be beaten entirely. However, it's worth trying.'

'Do you suppose he might have burned the cane too?'

Dickerson shook his head. 'Not a chance. If anyone had tried to burn a sword-cane in that furnace, your friend Sprague would be down here yet trying to extricate the clinker from the grates.' Dickerson sighed, chewing his moustache. Then: 'I don't feel quite as smart as I did a couple of hours ago when I put a few obvious marks together and made a cane out of them. I'm afraid we're up against a shrewd one, Boyle. This is going to be tough.'

8

Someone in Hartford must have decided that Dickerson needed additional help, for early on Saturday morning a man showed up. Theodore Kohler was an operative whom Dickerson knew and had worked with before. Kohler was slow-moving and slow-speaking, his general appearance unprepossessing. But Kohler was perhaps the best recovery man in New England. He had been responsible for the return of nearly a million dollars' worth of negotiable bonds that had mysteriously disappeared from the portfolio of an insurance company, and he had lately been instrumental in running to earth a tri-state gasoline coupon counterfeiting ring.

Dickerson counted himself extremely lucky, for in the job at hand he couldn't have asked for a better man.

They held a council of war in the Boyle kitchen. Sergeant Boyle, Kohler and

Perry Thompson were present, and the council was augmented by Boyle's father, the letter carrier, who had the day off. The old gentleman was more than interested in being there; he had a definite purpose, and his blue eyes, fiercely bright behind glasses, followed Dickerson's every move while he awaited his cue.

Swiftly and concisely, Dickerson outlined the progress thus far. He attempted no surmises and held nothing back. He began his outline from the beginning, which to his mind had now shifted to the Boston office of Dr. Julian Martens. For purposes of clarity, he had printed a list of names on a sheet of paper and had further prepared index cards, individually headed by each of the names.

His list, in the order in which he'd set it down, consisted of the names of Ben Sutts, Manuel Zella, Prudence Heath, Henry Heath, Frederick Thorne, Marion Kendall, Eugene Cotton Kendall, Harold Finch (he'd included that one because he had learned that Finch's wife and Marion Kendall were sisters, and also because Finch possessed a key to the basement door of the bank), William Stanczyk, and Carlos DeSylvia.

'I have listed Cotton Kendall and William Stanczyk,' Dickerson said, 'because we are faced with the definite possibility that, despite the fact no news of their recovery has been issued, one or both of these men may no longer be missing in action and may in fact have been in Sudwich on Thursday night. In this regard, Sergeant Boyle's father has some interesting evidence to add to our findings. Mr. Boyle, will you kindly repeat the details of the scene you witnessed in front of the post office on Wednesday morning?'

Postman Boyle leaned forward. 'It was a little after nine o'clock, and I was just starting my route. I had been in the post office, picking up my load, when Reba and Julie Johnson came in, and I heard them tell the stamp clerk that Henry Heath and his secretary Tessie Morgan were having a terrific argument outside in front of a stranger, a funny-looking man who was just like a scarecrow — that was the word Reba used. Reba and Julie were still at the stamp window when I went out, and when I came around the corner of the building to the front walk, Heath and Tessie Morgan had gone, but the stranger was still there.

'I don't suppose I'd have taken any notice of him if it hadn't been for Reba Johnson, but when I did look at him I had an odd feeling. I was sure I'd never seen him before in my life, yet it seemed like I ought to know who he was. So I stepped up to him and made some remark about the weather, and then I noticed he was looking at some red spots on the pavement where Tessie had spilled the nail polish that her row with Heath had been about.

'Well, this man started to answer me, but his voice wasn't like anything I'd ever heard before, and I couldn't make head nor tail out of what he was trying to say. And then all of a sudden old man Kendall's coupé pulled up to the kerb, and a fellow who looked like a wrestler — '

'That was DeSylvia,' Dickerson interrupted. 'Go on.'

'This DeSylvia got out, grabbed the

funny-looking fellow by the arm and said to him, 'We've been looking all over for you. Don't you ever do that again.' So this scarecrow-looking fellow went with him peaceable enough and got into the car and they drove off.'

'And who was driving the car?' Dickerson prompted.

'I'm almost positive it was Marion Kendall.'

Dickerson said, 'Thank you, Mr. Boyle. Now we are not attempting to establish the identity of this person as Cotton Kendall; until we have had a chance to interview the senior Kendall and Marion Kendall, we will accept only the fact of his presence and the company he was in. And that brings us up to date. Now, we've got to move fast and be absolutely sure of our moves. I am convinced that we are up against a killer of extraordinary cunning and shrewdness; it would seem that this person has anticipated the line our investigation would take and has left us a lot of false trails to follow. But this much should console us: while the list of names we have is large, it constitutes a circle, and somewhere within that circle will be our answer and our man or woman.

'Mr. Boyle, Senior has kindly volunteered his time to act as co-ordinator of our efforts. He will maintain a headquarters here and will receive and dispatch telephone calls to avoid needless cross-checking and duplication of efforts. For the purpose of convenience, you, Sergeant Boyle, and you, Perry Thompson, will work together. Your people will be Ben Sutts, Manuel Zella, Prudence Heath and Henry Heath. You, Kohler, will confine yourself for the present to Mr. Thorne. If it is possible to gain access to his studio without his knowledge, I want you to examine his trouser cuffs for particles of grain or meal dust, and examine the sleeves and front of his overcoat for bloodstains. But under no circumstances are you to go up against the man until I give you the word. I received a call from Julian Martens; he is coming to Sudwich this morning and will pay a visit to Thorne at his studio. Now, is all that clear?'

Kohler blinked sleepy eyes. 'What about the Stanczyk family?' he asked. 'Anyone checking on them?'

Sergeant Boyle answered, 'There isn't any. The mother's been dead for some years; old man Stanczyk died a few months after Bill joined the Marines. There weren't any other children.' Turning to his father, he asked, 'Pop, do you think that might have been Cotton Kendall you saw?'

'Well, he was wearing a green felt hat, and Cotton used to wear one of them. Could've been him, if he was all banged up like you say.'

'But you aren't sure. Might it have been Bill Stanczyk?'

'Possibly. But I don't think Stanczyk ever wore a hat, green or otherwise. And besides, if it was Stanczyk, what'd he be doing with Marion Kendall?'

Dickerson frowned. 'That, Mr. Boyle,' he said, 'is just one of the things we'd like to know.'

★   ★   ★

At the hectic breakfast in the Boyle household, Dickerson had been fortunate enough to pick up a name. And so, when Sergeant Boyle, Thompson and Kohler started off on their appointed rounds, leaving Pop Boyle as adjutant-in-charge, Dickerson began a walk until he found himself facing a little square and fenced-in house set well beyond the fashionable district of Mizzen Hill.

Here an old lady lived alone, and it wasn't too difficult for Dickerson to get himself invited inside. The old lady, whose name was Sturgis, was glad to have someone to talk to; she was deeply concerned by the horrible things that had been happening in Sudwich.

Mrs. Sturgis discovered in Dickerson a most interested and intelligent listener, and after he had sat in a Windsor chair and held two skeins of her yarn for the scarf she was knitting, they were fast friends.

Mrs. Sturgis had been the Eastlakes' housekeeper long before Sam Eastlake and his wife had perished in a disastrous ship's fire off the coast of New Jersey; that was in 1933, and they had been returning from a trip to Havana; that was three years before Isabelle had married Harold

Finch, and six years before Marion Eastlake had become Marion Kendall.

The Eastlake house had been the large square yellow one, the one with the widow's walk on the roof, next door to Ford Sheppard's on the Hill. Sam Eastlake had been connected with the mill, and he had been president of the bank, and was considered to be very well to do. But after he died, it began to appear that he'd never saved anything. Marion had tried her level best to keep the house up, but she'd had to let the servants go until just she and the old lady were left.

The last winter had been dreadful, Mrs. Sturgis said. She had been forced to dip into her own meagre savings so they could eat and try to keep warm. But Marion had paid her back, every cent, when she married Cotton Kendall. And Marion was helping her now, too. Every month as regular as the calendar a cheque came in.

The old lady had been surprised when Marion consented to become Cotton Kendall's wife. She had figured that maybe someday Marion and Ford Sheppard might hit it off. Of course, he was a lot older than she was, and he couldn't seem to settle down. But when Marion had come back from college in Northampton that first year, so grown up and really beautiful, Ford Sheppard had started to take notice of her. Maybe if he hadn't been in Nassau that awful last winter, getting his picture in the rotogravure section with some countess, the story might have been different.

But old man Kendall was pretty shrewd. The old man — funny how everyone had called him that ever since he was thirty years old, because he owned the mill, probably — well, the old man had arranged for Marion and Cotton to see an awful lot of each other. And Cotton was such a nice boy, and so handsome. Sometimes, maybe, he was moody and hard to understand — but there was no question about his worshipping the ground that Marion had walked on. It was such a shame that Cotton had gone off to war as a volunteer. The chances were he would never have been drafted, being a married man. People in Sudwich generally laid that to Mr. Thorne's influence. Mr. Thorne had been in the last war, and likely he'd filled the boy's head with a lot of his own peculiar ideals.

But Mr. Thorne was being paid back in kind now. People said he hardly ever came into the village any more except to buy a few groceries. And people said that he looked simply terrible, so haggard and drawn

Henry Heath? Yes, Henry was a local boy. He'd inherited the mill on River Street, the one that was now being used as a furniture storage warehouse. Henry hadn't done such a very good job of running his father's mill; he'd finally gone bankrupt, and it had been very generous of Mr. Kendall to give him a job. Henry had married Prudence Kendall — let's see, what year was it? Anyway, she had been close to thirty years old at the time, and everybody thought she was going to be an old maid.

★ ★ ★

Harold Finch glanced up with startled myopic eyes. Adjusting his tortoise-rimmed glasses nervously, he said, 'But,

Mr. Dickerson, what you suggest is highly irregular. I scarcely see how I could justify my position. You must know that there are certain ethics of banking which simply cannot be ignored.'

Dickerson, seated with Finch in the directors' room of the Sudwich First Bank and Trust Company, was rapidly becoming annoyed. He had been beating about the bush with this bald, myopic and skinny little vulture for the better part of half an hour.

'So's murder irregular, Mr. Finch,' Dickerson said bluntly. 'I can get a court order, yes. I can have it by tonight. But tonight you'll be closed; the time lock on your vault will be set and it won't release until Monday morning. Time, Mr. Finch, is important in this case. You may not appreciate the fact, but someone who has already murdered two people would scarcely hesitate at murdering one or more others.'

Mr. Finch twisted his thin fingers in alarm. 'I realize your viewpoint,' he said. 'But I simply cannot open Mr. Sheppard's box for you without a court order, even if you do have a key. I cannot take the responsibility.'

'And with Judge Hanley a pneumonia case in the hospital, the nearest court is New Haven. On whose responsibility would you open it?'

'Well, Mr. Cartwright, the president — '

'And you say he's in Florida!' Dickerson exploded. His moustache came in for a prolonged attack. Finally he said, 'All right. Guess there's nothing left but for me to go to New Haven.'

A lot of relief showed through and above Finch's tortoise-rimmed glasses. There was so much more relief than the occasion called for that Dickerson, who had been preparing to rise, settled down to fight. Very quietly he said, 'Sheppard was a pretty careless man, *apparently*, wasn't he?'

Finch froze. 'Careless? Do you mean about his personal habits?'

'I think you know what I mean.'

Finch laughed uneasily. 'He wasn't the world's best businessman, if that's what you mean. I've been trying for a long time to get him to sit down and revise his investment list. Some of his investments might have been very sound twenty years ago, but they could scarcely be called that in the light of present-day requirements.'

'You'd better close that door, Finch.'

The little man's jaw dropped. 'The door?' he repeated vaguely.

'Yes. Close it. Unless you want the whole bank to hear.'

Finch's cheeks flushed. 'Really, Mr. Dickerson. I believe you're trying to threaten me. This is quite absurd!'

'Would you think it absurd if I told you that Sheppard kept a complete and minute inventory of every item in his safe deposit box? And would you still consider it absurd if I told you that listed in that inventory was an unrecorded mortgage for four thousand dollars on the home of Emily Finch, that he had a notation which showed the mortgage to be past due and arrears, and that he had every intention of foreclosing it?'

Finch got up hastily and closed the door. When he returned to his seat, stark terror showed in his eyes. 'Please, Mr. Dickerson . . . '

Dickerson sat without speaking. His

mouth was set in a grim line, and there was no pity in his florid face.

Finch tortured his fingers. 'I suppose you think my refusal to open the box is based on a presumption that this mortgage . . . ' He paused, expecting assistance from Dickerson. But he didn't get any. 'You think that I, the cashier of the bank . . . '

Finch drew a handkerchief from his pocket, removed his glasses and wiped them with shaking hands. Wiping his eyes and forehead with the handkerchief he returned it to his pocket and returned the glasses to his nose. 'I was performing a service for Mr. Sheppard,' he said in a thin, frightened voice. 'He was involved in a deal in which he stood to make a lot of money. We spent most of the day on it Thursday, and it was understood that I would be paid for my services, and that the payment would approximate the mortgage on my mother's home.

'Mr. Sheppard had proceeded so far with the deal as to borrow on security twenty thousand dollars in cash which he took with him when he left the bank at five o'clock Thursday afternoon. It was my understanding that he was to meet his principal Thursday evening and that the deal would then be consummated. So that meant my part in it was done. My services had been performed, and therefore my payment would be due.'

Finch removed his handkerchief once more and wiped his streaming forehead. 'So when I learned of his death, I felt that I would be cheated. I had required no contract of him; his orders to me had been verbal; I would have nothing to show that I had performed the work he asked. Yet I had done my work carefully, faithfully and well and he had expressed complete satisfaction in it. And so . . . ' Finch exhaled and sat staring at his hands.

'And so you paid yourself by lifting your mother's mortgage from his effects,' Dickerson said. His mask held, but inwardly he was exultant. 'What was this work you did for him that was worth four thousand dollars?'

The ghost of a smile appeared on Finch's thin lips. 'I do not say that the work was worth four thousand. That is the sum he had agreed to pay. It consisted of preparing a complete financial statement on Henry Heath. It necessitated calls to financial institutions in Boston, New Haven and Hartford, where Heath has large loans against securities. I was also required to prepare a detailed financial statement of the Kendall-Sudwich Mills, of which Mr. Heath was manager.'

Dickerson's snapped: 'You say that he carried out twenty thousand in cash from here? It wasn't at his house, or Boyle would have reported it. And it wasn't on him when the body was found.'

'He took it with him. I have his note, and a receipt for the cash.'

'And who was Sheppard dealing with that he wanted to know so much about Heath?'

Finch smiled faintly. 'He was dealing with Heath.'

Some new thoughts about the fat little man and his plain and rather annoying wife crossed Dickerson's brain. 'I assume that this big deal Sheppard was contemplating had something to do with the Kendall-Sudwich mills. Just what was the nature of it?'

'I believe they were planning to seize control.'

'But Heath is already the manager, and he's Kendall's son-in-law. Why would he want any more control?'

'I'm afraid Mr. Heath will have to answer that. Perhaps it was because he feared that, with Mr. Kendall so ill, control might fall into outside hands.' Finch had recovered from his alarm and a note of confiding intimacy crept into his voice. 'It happens that I am connected with the Kendall family by marriage; Marion Kendall is my wife's sister, and so I thought it strange that Mr. Sheppard would come to me, of all people, with a scheme to take over the mill. But he was quite open and frank with me. He said that whatever steps he was taking were to protect Marion's interests. You see, they had been next door neighbours for years, and with Marion's husband a war casualty — Cotton has been missing for five months or more — his interest in her affairs was understandable. Especially since I believe he was quite fond of her.'

Dickerson frowned. 'Did you check

with Mrs. Kendall, to verify his claim of representing her?'

'No. He had asked me to keep the matter in confidence.'

'And you didn't call Kendall himself? It seems to me he would be the person most vitally interested in any plans to gain control of his mill. It looks to me as though his apparent heirs have been acting in mighty indecent haste, trying to divide up his property amongst themselves.'

'Since his tragedy, Mr. Kendall had lost all interest the business — all interest in everything. He is a director of this bank, and I have attempted to telephone him several times on important matters of policy, and each time he has told me quite plainly that he wished to be left alone.'

That helped to bring sense to some of it in Dickerson's mind, but it still didn't whitewash what had definitely appeared to be a conspiracy. Finch had said that Sheppard stood to make a great deal of money; if his sole desire had been to protect Marion Kendall, Ford Sheppard wouldn't have entered the deal to make money.

That thought opened up an entirely new and stunning possibility. Soberly, Dickerson asked, 'Finch, do you suppose that Sheppard was preparing to double-cross Heath and seize control of the mill for himself?'

An odd light entered Finch's myopic eyes. 'There wasn't the slightest doubt of it in my mind from the moment I first realized just why Mr. Sheppard wanted the reports,' he said firmly. He dropped his voice to a confidential level, 'And there's something else I think you ought to know. As I told you, I had contacted various banks on Thursday to secure the latest available information for a financial state-ment on Mr. Heath. Yesterday afternoon Chauncey Applegate, cashier of the New Haven Commercial, called me on the tele-phone and told me that Heath had been in at eleven in the morning and had depos-ited twenty thousand to his account.'

Dickerson stood up. 'That mortgage,' he said sternly. 'I expect to find it among the other effects when we inventory

Sheppard's safe-deposit box on Monday morning.'

* * *

'This is it. One-twenty-six, Pond Mills Road,' the taxi driver said. 'That's the Tolbert's place right up there.' So Dickerson got out, and as he was paying the driver a thought struck him. He asked, 'Do you know Mrs. Marion Kendall by sight?'

The driver nodded vigorously. 'Sure do. Known her all her life. It was her father, Sam Eastlake, set me up in business.'

'Have you had occasion to render taxi service for her recently?'

'Sure have. Took her to the two-fifteen for Boston Thursday afternoon and picked her up again at the station at midnight. She'd come in on the late train.'

'You're sure this was on Thursday?'

'Positive. Day before yesterday, the day Ford Sheppard was killed. My boy had to come up to the square to get me. I was up there with everybody else.'

'Did you tell Mrs. Kendall that Sheppard had been murdered?'

'I did. Figured she'd like to know. They was neighbours for years.'

'How did she react when you told her?'

'She was shocked, just like everybody else. Want me to wait?'

'No, thanks. I'll walk back.'

The driver started up and Dickerson turned to climb the winding drive. The Tolbert residence was set perhaps a hundred or more yards from the road, but Dickerson had requested to be put down at the gate so as to give the occupants full time to prepare for him. And as he climbed slowly he admiringly inspected the spacious and square white-clapboard house with its Grecian columns set in a wide porch. It was built on a knoll overlooking a small pond, and beyond were the rolling waters of Long Island Sound.

Dickerson reached the porch, punched the bell and stood back, hat in hand. A smartly dressed young woman answered the bell, surveyed him carefully, and in a thoroughly cool voice asked, 'Yes?'

'I presume you are Mrs. Tolbert,' Dickerson said smoothly. 'I understand that Mrs. Kendall is spending the day with you. I'd like to see her, please.'

The young woman eyed him. 'I don't believe Mrs. Kendall would care to see anyone right now.'

Dickerson smiled. 'I can quite understand. But I'm afraid there isn't much choice in the matter.' And he opened his palm to reveal a badge.

The young woman said, 'Good heavens!' and then she stepped aside to let him in. Indicating a pleasant living-room, she said, 'Go in and sit down. She's upstairs.' Mrs. Tolbert paused. 'Is this necessary? Marion's been having rather a hard time of it.'

'I assure you that it is very necessary.'

Dickerson seated himself. A few moments later he heard footsteps, and rising, turned to face Marion Kendall. All his preconceived notions were swept away. The young woman who walked so calmly in had poise and she had candour.

'I understand you wish to see me?' Her voice was pleasant, containing no hint of other than the most cursory curiosity.

'I don't like to bother you, Mrs.

Kendall, but perhaps my visit may save you a lot of later embarrassment.'

She looked inquiringly at him, and indicated a deep leather chair. 'Won't you sit down?'

Dickerson sat, balancing his hat on his knee, and watched her as she composedly arranged herself on a wide low-backed settee. Standing or sitting, he decided, she was the most stunning thing he had ever seen.

'I suppose you want to ask me about Ford Sheppard,' she asked calmly.

'I do. You can answer some questions for me. If you answer them satisfactorily, I'm sure it won't be necessary to annoy you further.'

He was totally unprepared for her next statement. 'I have been in love with Shep since I was ten,' she said. 'Of course at that time he was twenty-five, and totally unaware of my presence. He was very busily engaged in attempting to spend all the money his father was foolish enough to give him. It seemed utterly hopeless until I returned from my freshman term at college. That year, I think, he might have asked me to marry him if I hadn't chased him so brazenly.'

Dickerson moved uneasily from the spell of her voice. His eyes looked away and he said: 'I hadn't quite expected this to be a confessional, Mrs. Kendall. I only wanted to ask you a few questions.'

'I believe you also expressed a desire to save me embarrassment,' she said crisply. 'I fully realize the consequences to me of Sheppard's murder. There are certain things about us that will come to light. In the eyes and minds of many people of Sudwich, these things will be unpleasant, perhaps downright nasty. But I believe that you are sufficiently mature and experienced to know that there are certain circumstances surrounding our lives which all of us are not always able to recognize or understand. For my part, I know that I found myself enmeshed in a web of circumstances which made my actions with Ford Sheppard seem, even to me, entirely unexplainable, and a further continuance of our relationship impossible.'

'I hope you realize what you are saying, Mrs. Kendall,' Dickerson said. 'I didn't come here asking you to put yourself on the spot.'

'You mean in regard to Shep's death?' She shrugged impatiently. 'I am well aware that you are an officer of the law and that it is your job to find out who did this thing. What I am saying is in confidence, an attempt to justify those actions of mine which to you may have seemed so unjustifiable. You know that I am a married woman, and unless you are a very poor detective you will have heard of an 'affair.' But you probably would not know that I married Cotton Kendall realizing that I did not love him; that I loved Shep and would doubtless always continue to do so. We drifted a long time, Cotton and I. Oh, I tried hard. I liked Cotton. He was finer, cleaner and in countless ways a better man than Shep could ever be. But a man of your position must know that the heart of a woman is a strange and unpredictable thing.

'Perhaps I should tell you of my father-in-law's position in our lives. It was he more than anyone else who was responsible for my marriage to Cotton,

257

although he knew and has always known every one of my innermost secrets. He knew that I was in love with Shep when I married his son, and he knows that I have held clandestine meetings with Shep in these past few months. But he has never mentioned it and he never will; that, in a measure, is his punishment for me because he realizes that I had willingly allowed myself to become entrapped in a loveless marriage in exchange for security.'

Marion Kendall's head dropped down. 'After Cotton volunteered and was accepted for flight training in the Marine Corps, I began, quite unreasonably, to see a lot of Shep . . . all very innocent and neighbourly. Little visits across the hedge; little moments at parties we both attended. I kept fighting my desire to see him, to throw myself in his way, but I knew I was licked. And then Cotton was reported missing in action.'

Her eyes came up and fixed steadily on Joe Dickerson. 'You can never know how inadequate those words are. In the beginning, they could mean but one thing to me. Cotton was dead, and I was free.

There was nothing to keep me from Ford Sheppard now, and that is the part of which you shall hear. It will start in a whisper and will grow like a storm.' Her head dropped down again.

Dickerson soberly regarded his shoes. 'You did not realize, then, that you were not quite so free as you thought.'

Her head came up quickly. Her face was suddenly white and strained. 'You've been to see Mr. Kendall? You know, then, about Cotton?'

'I don't know nearly as much as I would like to know. That was my purpose in coming here today, to learn what you knew about his supposed return.'

She stiffened. 'Why do you say his 'supposed' return? Do you think that, had I been informed two months ago when my father-in-law first received the news of Cotton's safety, I would have continued my meetings with Shep? I may have been a foolish woman, but I am not a bad one.'

'I don't know, Mrs. Kendall. That's what I am trying to find out. When did you first learn that your husband was no longer missing?'

'On Wednesday morning, when a man, a male nurse, brought him to the house. That was my first realization of the fact that he was even alive.'

Dickerson stared in disbelief. 'Do you mean to tell me that you weren't notified? That your father-in-law kept this knowledge from you for two months?'

'I can assure you.' Her voice was low and bitter. 'You have only to ask Mr. Kendall if you choose not to believe me.' Dickerson felt the hair rise on the back of his neck. 'What in heaven's name could the man have been thinking of?'

'You don't know Mr. Kendall. He has never done a purposeless thing in his life. His purpose was to punish me because he knew that I had been seeing Shep.'

Dickerson sat back, shaking his head. 'The man must be mad. Certainly he must have realized that his son would have ultimately learned of your affair with Sheppard. Tell me, what occurred when your husband saw his father on Wednesday morning? What did they say to each other?'

'Cotton didn't see his father,' she

answered quietly.

'Why not?'

She began to show her tension now. It began to creep through her shell.

'Naturally I was shocked,' she said tautly. 'I was alone downstairs. Amy had gone to market, and father Kendall's nurse was giving him his morning bath, when they came. I shall never forget that moment so long as I live. The house faces east, and the morning sun was behind them when I opened the door. Suddenly, I can't explain how, I knew who he was. After that first glance, I could not look at him, he — he was so terribly changed. We entered the living-room and sat down. Cotton did not face me; he did not even seem to know me. The man with him kept chattering the most stupid things, about what a great moment this must be; how long he had looked forward to this moment, over and over like a senseless parrot. Then he wanted to see father Kendall right away, to complete the homecoming.

'I at last realized that this man — his name was DeSylvia — was talking to me. I gathered my senses enough to tell him how desperately ill Mr. Kendall was, and how I thought he should be prepared for the shock — ' She broke off and squarely faced Dickerson. 'You must believe,' she said, 'that in that moment, I thought father Kendall was ignorant of Cotton's being alive. He had told me nothing, and so I assumed that he knew nothing. My actions then were to spare him the horror of seeing the mutilated shell that had returned to him. I felt that he had waited so long he could wait a few weeks more, and so in my desperation a plan came to me.

'I recalled a friend, a plastic surgeon named Julian Martens, who had occupied a summer cottage on the dunes. I remembered the miracles this surgeon had wrought, and it was my desperately formed plan to have my husband go to him, to be at least partially restored before facing his father. Believe me, in that moment I held no anger, no resentment, nothing but pity for the sick old man who had waited so long and with such seeming hopelessness.

'When I presented this plan, I fear that I hurt Cotton, because he got up and walked silently from the room. But DeSylvia agreed to it with enthusiasm. DeSylvia said he had notified father Kendall to expect their arrival, and that was the first inkling I had that Cotton's return was not a complete surprise. But DeSylvia rushed on: he would go to Boston, would make the necessary arrangements, would call Mr. Kendall from there, making some sort of excuse for non-appearance. For my part, I was to continue in apparent ignorance until such time as father Kendall should choose to tell me.

'And then we discovered that my husband had wandered away from us; had left the house while we were talking together, and was nowhere to be found.' Marion Kendall drew a long breath. 'I was desperately frightened. We got out the car, DeSylvia and I, and went in search of him. We had not far to go. We found him in front of the post office, talking to a letter-carrier. DeSylvia induced him to enter the car and we drove to the bus station.' She paused.

When she resumed, her voice was huskily low. 'In all that time, Cotton and I had not spoken a word to each other. I could not bear it to look at him; what had happened to him made me feel terribly cheap and unimportant. So we waited for the bus, and as we waited DeSylvia talked endlessly. He would call me from Boston; I was not to worry; I could have utmost confidence in him. At last the bus arrived, and I returned alone to face my father-in-law.'

'Did you tell him,' Dickerson asked, 'that you had seen Cotton?'

'No. The duplicity I had planned with DeSylvia proved unnecessary. Father Kendall called me into his room and calmly revealed that he had known of Cotton's safety for two months, that he had sent DeSylvia to California to accompany him home, that they would soon arrive, and that if I had any 'unfinished business' I had better tend to it.

'Can you realize how this brutal revelation served to add further to my distress? The rest of that day passed as in a horrible dream. I had arranged to meet Shep that night. I planned just what I would tell him, even rehearsed the words

I would say. But for some strange reason, he too was undergoing an emotional strain. He talked steadily, brushing aside my feeble attempts. He reviewed our situation completely and clearly. He intended, he said, to contact a friend in Washington to have Cotton declared legally dead. And then he asked me to marry him.' She turned her face away.

Dickerson contemplated his shoes. 'I take it that your attempt to inform Mr. Sheppard was not a complete success.'

'I failed miserably. I got as far as suggesting that Cotton could still be alive, that he might be hurt and needing me. But that was as far as I was able to go.'

'But you didn't see Sheppard after that?'

'No. He had dropped me in Mizzen Hill Road, and I was walking towards the gate when I realized that he had insisted that I meet him the following night. And then I saw Fred Thorne's station wagon coming down the drive from the house. I was so surprised, and, under the circumstances, so unnerved that I forgot all else.'

'You say Thorne was there? At what

time was this, Mrs. Kendall?'

'I am not sure. I know it was very late — we had talked a long time. Since Fred seldom visited the house, I guessed that he might have heard from Cotton and reported to father Kendall. I'm not sure that he saw me, for I walked on up the road and approached the house from the rear.'

'Did Mr. Kendall mention Thorne's visit?'

'Yes, the following morning. DeSylvia had finally telephoned me, and when I entered the bedroom to tell father Kendall that I was going to Boston, he said that Cotton had been in Thorne's studio the previous night.'

Dickerson frowned. 'That would be Wednesday night. But you had put both your husband and DeSylvia on the Boston bus Wednesday morning. If Cotton had wanted to see Thorne, why hadn't he done so while he was still in Sudwich? Why did he go to Boston first?'

'I don't know, Mr. Dickerson. Possibly he did not go directly to Boston. The bus makes a rest stop of fifteen minutes at

East Sudwich, and while there he might have decided to return.'

'What was the nature of DeSylvia's Thursday morning telephone call?'

'He was having some trouble, he said, in getting Dr. Martens to accept Cotton as a patient, and he thought that my intervention might help. I reached the city at shortly after four o'clock and went directly to the Swann Clinic. Dr. Martens asked me a great many questions, which I answered as best I could.

'I had understood DeSylvia to say that he would meet me in Dr. Martens' office, but he was not there when I arrived. He had failed to tell me where he and Cotton were staying, and Martens either could not or would not give me any information. And further, Martens both confused and frightened me by voicing distrust of DeSylvia: what did I know of the man? How had I come to hire him? What were his references?

'I did not know what to do. I telephoned Alice Wentworth, a woman I had known in college, and we had dinner together at Schrafft's. I explained some of my problem to her, and she suggested that DeSylvia might have taken Cotton to a private nursing home. She told me that I was upsetting myself about what had probably been a simple misunderstanding, that she would help me by telephoning hotels and hospitals if I desired it, and that I should return to Sudwich and wait until DeSylvia called again.

'I reached South Station too late for the early train, and so I spent wretched hours telephoning every possible place I could find listed in the directory. My results were nothing. On the train ride to Sudwich I was confused, depressed and becoming distrustful of both Dr. Martens and DeSylvia.

'And then, when I was riding home in the taxi, Jep Prince told me that — that Shep . . . '

Dickerson arose and walked quietly to a window and stood there looking out at the sparkling little pond, the rolling green-brown fields and the distant Sound, but he saw none of it. He remained for quite some time, turning things over in his mind, while he waited for her to regain her control.

He turned when he heard the sound of her match as she lighted a cigarette. 'Mrs. Kendall,' he asked, 'are you quite satisfied that the man, this scarecrow with DeSylvia, is your husband? You didn't talk to him, nor he to you. Beyond that first glance, in which you instinctively felt that he must be your husband, you scarcely looked at him. All you had to go on was the word of DeSylvia, who might well be a swindler. And on that day, Wednesday, you were in a condition bordering upon complete shock.

'You were unable,' Dickerson continued in a quiet voice, 'to contact your husband in Boston on Thursday, and you remained here in Sudwich yesterday. Under these circumstances, how can you be sure?'

She did not respond at once. She was looking, with eyes that held traces of pain, down the long avenues of memory. Then: 'I can tell you why I am sure. When he first arrived at the house, I cannot tell you what kind of a hat he was wearing; I cannot remember if he was wearing one at all. But for nearly two years there has been a faded green felt hat of his hanging in the coat closet in the hall. It was his favourite, and was awaiting his return. And when DeSylvia and I found him at the post office, he had it on.'

★   ★   ★

The sweatered railway express agent was attempting, by means of a paste-brush, to dig himself out of a mountain of boxes when Dickerson dropped in. The brush did not pause in its rapid movements as the agent asked, 'Ready for that ticket now?' And, with a special flourish, 'still got plenty of time for the two-fifteen.'

Dickerson sidestepped to protect his overcoat. 'No, I'm not quite ready yet. I'd like to find out if Marion Kendall has purchased a ticket for Boston recently.'

'Marion Kendall? She did. Bought one on Thursday. Round trip.' The relentless brush attacked a new pile. 'She used it, too. Left on Number Seven, at two-fifteen. She got on with Reba and Julie Johnson. Julie's got to have glasses.'

The agent ran out of materials and started for the counter. Midway, he stopped and turned. 'Say, a ticket's good for ninety days.'

And so Dickerson relented and made a purchase, although the return half of his ticket purchased in South Station still remained in his wallet. And Dickerson had reason to be glad that he did, for while he was waiting for the agent to unlock the enormous padlock, he was forcibly seized with an idea.

When Dickerson left the station, his usually florid face was quite pale, and his moustache was suffering a prolonged attack.

★   ★   ★

Back at the Boyle house, Dickerson learned that Tessie Morgan's car had been found abandoned in a vacant lot near the lumber yard. Vandals had removed the tyres and syphoned out the gasoline. The car was a disappointment, for the most careful search had failed to reveal any blood spots, fingerprints or traces of grain or meal dust.

9

It was two o'clock when Swayle's car turned in at the gates and crawled up the steep, straight drive to the Kendall mansion.

As the car came to rest in the spacious side yard, Swayle said: 'I don't like it, Dickerson. I know I'm a public official, but I'm also a physician, and Kendall is my patient. He has very bad angina. I'm not sure just how much excitement he can stand.'

Dickerson said, 'I had hoped that it wouldn't be necessary to bother him, but too many items have come up in which he is directly concerned. And I'm sure that if he survived a visit from Frederick Thorne last Wednesday night, he will suffer no ill results from this one.'

'I see your point,' Swayle admitted. 'But angina cases are funny. Sometimes the victim lingers for months, even years, and then again . . . ' He spread his hands.

Dickerson drew his dog-eared memo book from his pocket and consulted it. 'I think I'll let you handle the questions,' he said. 'According to telegraph office records, on January tenth you delivered to him the telegram of notification that his son had been found.'

Swayle flushed. 'I did,' he admitted. 'And I didn't mention it because Kendall had requested my confidence. He was very careful to explain his reasons, and while I didn't exactly see eye to eye with him, I felt that as a physician I had no alternative. Since, however, you seem to have discovered the fact, and since you appear to believe . . . ' He paused in annoyance. Dickerson evidently hadn't been listening to him, for he had been busily writing on a leaf in the memo book. When Dickerson had read what he had written, chewing vigorously at his moustache in the meanwhile, he tore the leaf from the book and then glanced up with a little start.

'I'm sorry,' Dickerson said. 'I'm afraid I wasn't listening. You were saying?'

'Practically nothing,' Swayle answered

in a sour voice. 'What's that you were writing?'

'The questions I would like you to ask Mr. Kendall.' Dickerson handed him the leaf.

Swayle glanced at it, and his round face became red. 'What's this — 'How did you happen to employ Carlos DeSylvia?' Why, he employed DeSylvia because I recommended him! Kendall wanted someone to go to the coast and accompany his son home, so he asked me for suggestions.'

'So you suggested DeSylvia. What do you know of the man?'

Swayle frowned. 'I had known him for some eight or ten years in New Haven, before I moved to Sudwich. I knew him to be reliable, and because of his strength, particularly well equipped to handle a case of this sort.'

'Why do you say 'because of his strength'? Did you have reason to believe that Cotton might become violent?'

'The telegram told us he was suffering from amnesia. You never know what to expect in a case like that. I thought it best not to take any chances.'

'In your opinion, then, DeSylvia was the best man for the job?'

'Well . . . ' Swayle hesitated. 'I believe I suggested several others, but at the time they were busy on cases. There's nothing really wrong with DeSylvia except that he is entirely too agreeable to any suggestion that comes along, especially if it comes from the people who are paying him.'

Dickerson grinned. 'All right, you can cross off the first question. I think we'd better be getting on in. Martens should be through by the time we are, and I still haven't heard from Connelly.'

They left the car, and on reaching the porch, Dickerson raised the heavy knocker and brought it sharply down.

At length the door opened as far as its chain would permit, and a voice said: 'I'm sorry, but Mr. Kendall is a very sick man and he won't see — why, it's Doctor Swayle!'

'Good afternoon, Amy.'

'Land's sakes, just a minute. I'll let you in.'

Following a rattle of the chain, the door opened wide. The tiny, aged guardian of the house took their coats and hats and said, 'He's not very good today, Doctor. If you hadn't come now, in another hour I would have called you anyway. He's awful upset about something.'

Her anxious yet curious eyes took in the impressive height and breadth of Dickerson, but she asked no questions. Evidently she took him for a consulting specialist whom Dr. Swayle had seen fit to bring along.

They found the old man in bed, being read to by an attractive nurse. This was Dickerson's first glimpse of the tycoon of Sudwich, and while he was shocked he was also in a way satisfied. Here was an old man who would never leave that room save in death.

Swayle exchanged eye signals with the nurse and then told her to get a breath of fresh air, a suggestion which she accepted with alacrity. And then Swayle went to the bed, gave a frowning glance at the chart hanging from the foot of it, and taking the old man's thin grey wrist in his strong hands, read his pulse.

The old man's eyes opened, vaguely

inspected Swayle, and swept beyond to Dickerson. Abruptly his eyes became hard. 'Who are you and what do you want?'

'Lieutenant Dickerson asked if he could come with me,' Swayle answered. 'He's been assigned to the Morgan and Sheppard cases.'

The old man inspected Dickerson curiously. 'Tessie was a good woman,' he said. 'Sheppard was a crook. If you find who killed him, give 'em a medal. But if you find who killed Tessie, give 'em the works.' He closed his eyes briefly. 'Why do you want to see me?'

Swayle released the thin wrist, returned his watch to his pocket, coughed and said, 'Lieutenant Dickerson requested me to ask you a few questions. Under the circumstances, I didn't feel that you should be subjected to — '

'Then why doesn't he ask 'em?' the old man interrupted impatiently. 'Go ahead, ask me. I've been worse than this and have managed to pull through.' He turned bleakly hostile eyes on Swayle. 'You go over there and sit down,' he ordered. 'If I was a doctor and couldn't do any better job on a patient than you've done on me, I'd give up.'

Somewhat red of face, Swayle marched to a chair and sat in it.

'Now, young man, what is it you want to ask me?'

Dickerson pulled a chair nearer to the bed and sat down. 'It won't be necessary for you to answer any question you don't want to. If you dislike the question, say 'pass' and I'll try another. All right?'

The old man leered at Swayle. 'You see? He's got a damned sight more sense than you have. All right, fire away.'

'Are you satisfied that the man DeSylvia brought here from San Diego is your son, Cotton?'

'I wasn't at first, but I am now.'

'Why weren't you at first?'

'Because to my mind he was never properly identified. It could just as easily have been his gunner Bill Stanczyk that the natives found. It could have been my son who was dead.'

'And why did you change your mind?'

'Because Fred Thorne came to me

Wednesday night and told me that Cotton had been in his studio. He said Cotton stood behind a screen, so he didn't actually see him. But he did say that he talked with him for a long time and was quite satisfied as to his identity . . . ' The old man's voice faltered, but only for an instant. 'My son was deeply attached to Thorne, and would not have wanted to reveal himself in his present state of disfiguration.'

'Just what proof did Thorne offer that his unseen guest was actually your son?'

'Cotton identified himself by recalling events from the past, things that had taken place when he was a boy, just after his mother died, and Thorne was a newcomer in Sudwich.'

Dickerson frowned thoughtfully. 'It would seem, then, that your son had recovered from his amnesia?'

'Apparently so, unless Thorne was manufacturing the story out of whole cloth, and I see no reason why he would. I believe that he acted in the best of faith.'

'Mr. Kendall, would you mind telling me why you withheld the information of

Cotton's return from his wife for so long?'

'Pass,' the old man said promptly.

Dickerson smiled. 'All right. Was it because you were aware of her infatuation for Ford Sheppard?'

'I — pass!'

'Do you think that Thorne might have known of the affair between your daughter-in-law and Ford Sheppard?' Dickerson asked in deadly serious voice, and then he added, 'You see, I realize that an extraordinary bond of affection existed between Thorne and your son. Thorne, being a highly idealistic person, might have taken it into his hands to remove Sheppard so that your son would not be forced to suffer any further than he had already suffered.'

A flicker of interest passed quickly through the old man's eyes. 'It's possible that he knew of the affair,' he said, and it was his first direct admission that he himself had known of it, 'but I hope for his own sake that he didn't take the course you suggest. While I haven't been on the friendliest terms with him, I'd hate to think of him jeopardizing himself for the removal of a rat like Sheppard. And as for Marion . . . ' He paused and his eyes took on reflective depths. 'Well, if Cotton hadn't come back, she'd probably have married Sheppard eventually.'

Dickerson leaned forward. 'Are you suggesting that Marion might have removed Sheppard because of Cotton's return?'

The old man shrugged. 'I'm not suggesting anything. It's no secret that there isn't any love lost between my daughter-in-law and me. I know her for just what she is. If it was love instead of money that kept her married to my son, why isn't she with him now in Boston instead of staying here with the Tolberts? He needs her; they don't.'

'Suppose she had tried to locate him in Boston, and had failed?'

The old man didn't answer immediately. His grey wrinkled face took on a look of infinite shrewdness.

'So you think,' the old man said, 'that maybe my son might have killed Ford Sheppard, eh? I'll admit there's a possibility. But answer me this: you're working on Tessie Morgan's murder, too, and if you're any good at all, you know by this time whether or not the same person killed both Ford Sheppard and Tessie. Now if it's true that you're looking for just one person, you can rub Cotton's name out. Unless Bill Stanczyk told him about her, he never even heard of the woman.'

Dickerson stood up. 'Thank you, Mr. Kendall,' he said. 'There's just one more question, and then I'll let you alone. Were you, or rather I should say the Kendall-Sudwich mill, in a position where anyone could do you a lot of damage?'

The old man smiled mirthlessly. 'I was,' he admitted. 'I was so wrapped up in thinking about my son that I had let the mill slide. But when I was satisfied that he was safe — that is, when Thorne satisfied me that he was safe — I began to get interested again because I wanted to be sure Cotton had something to come home to. So I found that Heath had let the dividends lapse on the preferred shares. That's taken care of now. The bond house that's doing the refinancing mailed the dividend cheques yesterday.'

★   ★   ★

Thorne was at his canvas when he heard the sound of a car approaching on the Dunes Road, slow down and swing into his driveway. The car came to a stop, footsteps crunched on the brick terrace, and a brisk knock sounded at his door.

'Come in!' he boomed, not deigning to turn around, and the draught from the door struck him full in the back.

'Mr. Thorne! I am so glad to find you here. I would have telephoned, except that I remembered: you never answer the telephone while you are working. So on a chance, I came.'

The painter turned slowly, and saw standing before him an aristocratic white-haired man dressed tastefully and expensively. He was smiling, a shy, engaging smile, and his eyes were twinkling.

'Oh, yes. I recognize your voice. You called me the other evening. Martens, isn't it?'

'Julian Martens. I am flattered that you knew me. I was — er — expecting a call from you yesterday. And then I realized how busy you must be, so I made the necessary arrangements.' He spread his hands. 'And here I am.'

Thorne deposited his brushes in the cracked pitcher next to the easel stand. 'Excuse me a minute while I clean up,' he said. 'Make yourself at home.' He made his dragging way to the kitchen, capturing a can of turpentine en route. Methodically he spilled a quantity of the spirits on his bony hands, rubbed them briskly, and then lathered them with soap. When he returned to the studio, drawing on his corduroy jacket as he came, he found his guest nodding at the easel.

'Beautiful,' Martens murmured. 'Such colour and depth. Such warmth and life! It is a masterpiece. You are indeed a gifted man, sir.'

'Thank you.' Thorne warmed to him. 'I hope to have it finished soon.'

'Finished! Is it not finished now?'

Thorne chuckled. 'Almost. It should be finished tomorrow.'

Martens reluctantly took his eyes from the painting. 'You know why I am here. The young man returned to me. I have accepted him as a patient; I think we shall do fairly well. I think I can help him.'

Thorne breathed out. Glancing around, he said, 'Here, have a chair — just dump that stuff on the floor.' They sat down, Martens in a straight-backed chair from which he had first carefully removed several small frames, and the artist in his rocker. Martens seemed about to speak on the subject of Cotton Kendall, and then his eyes clouded sympathetically.

'Do not think me rude,' he said, 'but it is the professional man in me. Your leg. It is so — so unfortunate that one so gifted as you should suffer such an affliction. You were injured in an accident, perhaps?'

Thorne smiled grimly. 'Not an accident. Infantile. It happened to me back in nineteen twenty-nine, along with a lot of other things.'

'Ah, the dread polio. A terrible thing. But you have risen above it. You are made of the good stuff. You learned to walk again with a crutch? Or a cane, perhaps?'

It was impossible not to like this man. 'I used a cane at first. For quite a long while, actually. It was rather a remarkable cane, an ebony affair inlaid with silver. It was reputed to at one time have been the property of Baron Rothschild. At least, that's the story I got from the fellow who sold it to me in a Sixth Avenue hock shop. There was a little trick catch near the head, and if you pressed it the cane fell apart — '

'Revealing a sword!' Martens breathed. 'A sword-cane belonging to the Baron Rothschild, once the richest man in the world!' His face became transfixed and his voice held pleading. 'You still have it, yes? You will let me see it? Believe me, sir, I am a collector of canes. I have more than a hundred. But a cane such as this . . .'

Thorne frowned. 'I'm just trying to remember where the blamed thing is.' He pushed himself up from the chair and stood undecided. 'Most likely,' he mused, 'it'll be in the dressing alcove. That's where everything winds up.' He limped to the lacquered screen and disappeared behind it, and the sounds of search issued from the recesses of the alcove.

Martens exhaled gently. Some of the colour departed from his face and the engaging twinkle disappeared from his eyes. His right hand slipped down until it rested on the hard outline of the automatic pistol in his overcoat pocket. And then his hand swiftly entered the pocket and closed over the stock; but his narrowed, calculating eyes did not once leave the lacquered screen.

Thorne returned, grinning. 'I remember now,' he said, chuckling. 'I loaned it to one of my models the other night. She was afraid of burglars or something. I'll get it back from her and send it to you, if you really want it.'

Martens was all smiles again. His right hand quit the overcoat pocket and came up waving. 'At the risk of being a nuisance, I shall inevitably remind you,' he said. 'I am an ardent, and sometimes annoying, collector.'

When Thorne was seated again, Martens began to talk — of his work, of what he hoped to do for Kendall, of other patients. But as the fluent and modulated tones fell from his lips, his narration became interspersed with adroit questions.

It was a job beautifully done, and one which Kohler, who was at that moment hidden in the studio's bedroom and engaged in a painstaking search of the artist's clothing and other personal effects, was long afterward to remember and remark upon with sincere admiration. Its abrupt finish was indicative of the personality of Martens, the surgeon who was also not only a psychologist but a superb actor as well.

'I shall do my work,' he promised. 'And now I have one small, foolish favour to ask of you.' A fountain pen and a square of card appeared, as if by magic, in Martens' hands. 'Your autograph. I collect them too — Ah! You are left-handed? The mark of genius!'

★　★　★

'You say he admitted owning such a cane?' Dickerson asked in disbelief.

'Positively,' Martens replied. 'Not only did he admit ownership, he went to the alcove to search for it. And then he recalled having loaned it to one of his models.'

'Tessie Morgan, of course,' Dickerson grunted. 'And he claimed that it was Cotton Kendall who was in his studio Wednesday night?'

'He was quite definite about it.'

'And he apparently knew nothing of Tessie Morgan's murder?'

'Nothing. He gave every indication that he expects her to return so that he may finish the painting tomorrow.'

'That just isn't possible, not in a town the size of Sudwich.'

Postman Boyle had been an interested listener, and at this he brought his chair forward and said, 'I beg your pardon, Lieutenant, but it is possible that Thorne doesn't know Tessie was killed. We didn't know ourselves until yesterday noon, and he don't come into town more than once a week, and nobody goes to see him. I wouldn't go so far as to say he doesn't know, but it is possible.'

'Possible,' Martens admitted, 'but — er — there is more here than meets the eye. You are up against a brilliant criminal.

Thorne is a brilliant man. I do not say that he . . . ' Martens ended his sentence by spreading his hands in a suggestive gesture.

Dickerson objected, 'I'll admit the evidence seems overwhelmingly against him, but why would he kill his model? It seems to me that her removal, before the painting was completed, would have caused him considerable inconvenience.'

'I saw the painting,' Martens countered. 'To my eye, the work of the model was done. He could have used any model to substitute for the little remaining work on shawl and background.'

'But why? For what motive?'

Martens shrugged. 'My dear Dickerson, surely your investigation must furnish the answer to that. I only say that the man is capable: he has the sufficient ego; he had a motive, at least in Sheppard's case — the strong motive of loyalty to a friend. And who shall deny that he had opportunity?'

Dickerson, with no immediate rejoinder to offer, sat quietly thinking. The artist was in a most unhealthy spot. His sword-cane had killed Tessie Morgan. His car had been parked in the square and he had been seen, either entering or leaving it, shortly after Ford Sheppard had been killed less than a block distant. Perry Thompson, a most observing and reliable witness, had heard a dragging sound and had seen a shadow move; combined, that might easily have been Frederick Thorne pulling his crippled leg across the gravelled driveway in the rear of the feed store. Further, an investigation of the records at Town Hall had disclosed that permits for .32 calibre pistols had been issued to both Ford Sheppard and Frederick Thorne.

And there was Kohler's report, telephoned from the pay-booth at the railroad station not ten minutes ago, that he had found grains of oats and dust of meal in the cuffs of a pair of Thorne's trousers.

But against these, there were three indisputable points in Thorne's favour: first, although Kohler had found grain and meal dust, he had found no bloodstains; second, Thorne's time, prior to ten o'clock, was now pretty well accounted for; third and by far the most important, the complete lack of motive.

Had the murder of Tessie Morgan been motiveless, introduced with the sole intent and purpose of confusing the investigation? Dickerson thought not. If such had been the case, why would the killer go to such lengths to make the murders appear the work of different persons? Would not the killer, rather, have used the same weapon in both instances, thus forcing a search for a tying motive which it would be impossible to find?

And if Ford Sheppard had possessed a pistol, for which he had a permit, where was that pistol? Was it the weapon that had killed him? Or should Dickerson now toss aside his game of patience with Frederick Thorne and close in, seize his pistol for ballistics tests . . .

He was interrupted by the ringing of the telephone. Postman Boyle scrambled to answer it. He returned with the information that the call was for Dickerson and seemed to be mighty important.

Dickerson entered the hall, automatically glancing at his watch to see that it was now four o'clock, and picked up the receiver. 'Dickerson,' he said.

And then he was calling excitedly to Postman Boyle to bring more notepaper and a fresh pencil, for this was the call he had been awaiting since the night before.

★　★　★

Connelly's first words were in the form of a question: 'Is that guy Martens with you?' And at Dickerson's affirmative response, he said, 'Well, don't let him get away. There's something awful damned fishy about this whole business.'

Dickerson glanced apprehensively over his shoulder and saw that Martens and the elder Boyle had their heads together over the kitchen table and were whispering in low tones. Dickerson said, 'All right. Let me have it.'

'First,' Connelly said, 'I ain't gonna tell you how I got all this stuff; that can come later when we got more time. But you can depend on it. And when you put in your report to the commissioner, you can tell him I ain't been to bed since the day before yesterday — '

'I understand, man! Get on with your report!'

'Okay. Now, on Wednesday, Cotton Kendall and this DeSylvia both visit the Swann Clinic, and Kendall stays in a room in the hospital and DeSylvia takes off and doesn't come back. On Thursday morning De Sylvia shows up, and he's got the picture that was painted by this Thorne, which he gives to Martens. Then Martens calls you in and gives you a long song and dance, and you shove off without saying yes or no. Then Thursday afternoon, Mrs. Cotton Kendall shows up and is pigeonholed with the doc for more than an hour, and when she leaves she don't know her husband is right there in the hospital, for she begins calling every hospital in town. Are you listening?'

'I'm listening,' Dickerson said grimly. 'You're quite sure of your days?'

'Positive. Cotton Kendall has been in the Swann Clinic hospital since one o'clock Wednesday afternoon, and he's still there. And I been looking all over greater Boston for him since I got your call yesterday noon.'

294

Dickerson's eyes, as they contemplated the bent white and distinguished head above the kitchen table, were quite hard and exceedingly angry. 'Go on,' he said.

'And what is more,' Connelly continued, 'this Martens has got a detective force which consists of two dames, and they have been on my neck ever since I walked into his office. But that is neither here nor there. I chased 'em both out to Marblehead on a phony lead while I tried to get some track on this DeSylvia. I finally turned him up in a furnished room on Huntingdon Avenue. The landlady said that DeSylvia rented the room Wednesday afternoon and went out about five o'clock and didn't come back until two in the morning. She said he was out all day and all night Thursday and didn't get back until yesterday noon. Yesterday noon he came from Martens' office, where he had been trying to catch up on some details; he told the woman at the desk that he'd had to go to New Haven because he'd got word that his mother was taken sick. He wanted to know if Cotton Kendal was okay and if Mrs.

Kendall had been round. He's at the Huntington Avenue address and has been there ever since except for a visit to the Swann Clinic this morning.'

Dickerson filed that in neat pockets in his brain. 'Any more of it?'

'Nothing that matters, except one of my contacts in the hospital says this Cotton Kendall is a complete amnesia case. He doesn't know if he's Cotton Kendall or Jonah's whale, or so he says.'

'Would it be possible,' Dickerson asked, 'for him to have left the hospital for any length of time Thursday night without being observed?'

'Possible,' Connelly said, 'because he's got a private room and the hospital is short of help. But it ain't any too probable.'

'All right,' Dickerson said. 'Now, here's your next assignment. Go to South Station and find out if any of the three bought tickets to Sudwich Thursday evening — there are only two possible trains, at seven and ten o'clock. You'll probably have to wait for the late relief to come on, and you can get some sleep in the meantime. But don't slip up on it.'

Connelly got the 'sleep' part of it, at any rate. He rang off with a yawning sigh.

When Dickerson came into the kitchen, he saw that Julian Martens was watching him. There was a twinkle in the surgeon's eyes, and a faintly repressed smile about his mouth.

'The report,' Martens said. 'Was it — er — satisfactory?'

'Eminently so,' Dickerson answered quietly.

Martens spread his hands. 'Good. And now, I presume,' he sighed, 'you are about to ask me a great many questions.'

'Not so many,' Dickerson said.

The twinkle in the surgeon's eyes faded. Concern occupied his distinguished face, and when he spoke again, his words came slowly. 'When I first appealed to you,' he said, 'I had no realization that my little puzzle would lead to murder. Frankly, I distorted the facts slightly — I knew about the Kendall family of course — and purposely coloured the patient's mental attitude, but in all sincerity I ask you to believe that I did so only because I wanted to enlist your aid. I spoke quite truthfully when I said that I was an admirer of yours; as you know, my hobby is criminology, and it has always been one of my greatest desires to be permitted to observe you at work. In fairness I ask you to recall that, while you did not actually refuse to assist me, you did give me what was tantamount to a refusal, and so until you called me last night I considered your part in the matter as closed.'

Martens exhaled gently. 'Of itself,' he continued, 'the puzzle which DeSylvia and his scarecrow presented me was sufficiently complex to delight the mind of any ardent amateur criminologist. My error was that I simply could not resist the temptation of getting to know you by enlisting your aid. If I have obstructed justice, I am sorry and will face the penalty.'

'What is this 'puzzle' you keep talking about?' Dickerson demanded.

'I could gain no information from the patient,' Martens replied promptly. 'He was suffering amnesia. But I could not trust DeSylvia. The puzzle grew when the patient's wife — and I know this woman — appeared at my office and with obvious sincerity answered my questions, yet apparently had no vaguest notion that the patient was then in my hospital. Why had not DeSylvia so informed her? I decided to wait for further investigation. The puzzle reached a climax in a few hours when my call to Frederick Thorne produced only the most evasive answers and a halfway promise to visit me, which he did not keep. I could sense only a conspiracy to foist an impostor on the Kendall family.'

There was genuine distress in the surgeon's eyes. 'I felt that you, having been told I was a summer resident here prior to the hurricane, would realize that I both knew and recognized the subject of the portrait. It had been my hope that this would serve to pique your curiosity and cause you to throw your whole energies to stop this conspiracy.'

'And why do you keep calling it a conspiracy?'

'Because the human wreckage brought to me by this DeSylvia was not Cotton Kendall.'

Dickerson leaned forward. His anger had vanished completely before an intense eagerness that leaped from his compelling eyes.

'How do you know?' he asked hoarsely.

Martens chuckled. 'My dear Lieutenant, an artist of the capabilities and meticulousness of this Thorne would scarcely have failed to notice and record the shape of his model's ears. One of them is shown quite plainly and in detail in the sketch — a small ear with a smoothly rounded top. The ears of the scarecrow whom DeSylvia brought me are larger in proportion to his head, and quite noticeably pointed.'

★ ★ ★

Martens had been gone but a few moments when the telephone began a siege that was to last an exhaustive half-hour. During it, Dickerson twice ran out of note paper and had to content himself with cramming his brain.

When at last he quit the telephone, it was to go to work under the interested eye of Postman Boyle. And when he had finally assembled the reports and filed them under their proper headings, he sat in absorbed contemplation of his material.

Kohler's report, from a contact in New York: Frederick Thorne, prior to 1929, an importer of coffee, tea and spice; no partners, firm well rated. Married New York 1921, divorced Reno 1928; no record of remarriage; no record of children. Arrested December 1928 (twice) charges of public intoxication; arrested January 1929, same charge plus attempted suicide; no previous records of arrest. Business caught in price slump and commodity squeeze; lost heavily in stock market October 1929. Contracted infantile paralysis November 1929. Sold business and moved to Sudwich April or May, 1930.

Kohler also reported that he had learned from maids in the Sheppard residence that Thorne visited there shortly after nine-thirty on Thursday night, asked for Ford Sheppard and learned that he had gone out and might be found at the Dunes Club. The maid said Thorne appeared very clean and was not wearing gloves.

According to the Dunes Club bar tender, Sheppard arrived some time after nine-thirty, had one drink, kept to himself and made no telephone calls, and then departed. Thorne missed him there by a matter of moments. Thorne looked clean, but the bar tender could not recall if he was wearing gloves.

Statement of Barney Wurtzel, 9 King Street: 'I had just let the sitter out and was turning off the porch light when I saw Sheppard's coupé turn into the street from the Post Road, cross and turn down into Mizzen Hill Road toward Liberty Street. That was about ten minutes to ten.'

(Note: Ford Sheppard's actions during evening prior to murder now completely accounted for.)

Statement of Terrence Dugan, proprietor of Dugan's Cut Rate Store: 'I closed up the shop at a little before ten and crossed the square, on my way home. At that time Mr. Thorne was sitting in his station wagon in front of the bank. So far as I could see, he was alone.' (Question: Did you hear the shot? Answer: No. I was in my house by ten o'clock, so it must have been five minutes of ten when I saw Mr. Thorne.)

Kohler also reported the afternoon visit

of Martens to Thorne's studio; Thorne had been walking on the dunes shortly before, which gave Kohler opportunity to enter the studio. He (Kohler) did not reveal himself to Martens, nor had Martens been informed that Kohler was covering Thorne. Kohler's report, however, completely substantiated Martens' report.

Kohler said that in addition to the grain and meal particles in Thorne's cuffs, he had found a quantity on the floor of the station wagon. But there was no evidence of blood to be found anywhere either on Thorne's clothing or the station wagon.

Kohler made his report from the pay telephone on the station platform, from which he commanded a good view of the Dunes road. It took him forty-five minutes, Kohler said, to walk to the station by the Dunes road, and only twelve minutes by the railway bridge. Other than Martens, Thorne had had no visitors during the period of watch, which would continue until otherwise ordered.

Sergeant Boyle's report (including details by Perry Thompson): No metal particles or leather ash found in refuse of

Sudwich bank. Deposited contents of cans located by Ben Sprague, janitor. Sprague further stated that he had found no more mess than usual when cleaning up the bank restrooms on Friday morning. Sprague admitted, however, to mopping the basement floor, a daily procedure inaugurated by Mr. Finch.

From Perry Thompson: Lester Coe, proprietor of Coe's Tavern, opposite Kessler's store. Could not recall seeing anyone enter or loiter about alley leading to Tessie Morgan's apartment entrance on Thursday night. Coe did remember the presence of Ben Sutts on the previous night (Wednesday) and had notice that Sutts appeared upset. Coe did not see Sutts at all on Thursday night.

Manuel Zella, fisherman employed by Sutts. Came in Thursday night on the *Tessie M* at six-thirty, assisted in making fast to the pier and unloading the haul. Went home and cleaned up. Walked to Coe's Tavern, ate two sandwiches and drank two glasses of beer. Was leaving Coe's Tavern at eight o'clock when he saw a woman enter alley beside Kessler store.

Crossed street and recognized her as Mrs. Prudence Heath, and saw that she entered door leading up to Miss Morgan's apartment. Proceeded to Polish-American club one block distant where he caught Sutts before he mounted the platform, and reported the incident. Manuel Zella said Sutts told him to mind his own business, that he was no longer interested in Miss Morgan.

Manuel sat in end seat third row from back (corroborated by Walter Damon and Edgar Spruance) and listened to speeches until after ten o'clock, when man came in from Cataract Hose Company next door to call out all volunteer firemen. Manuel wasn't one, but he went out anyway because Sutts had just finished his speech. He learned at the fire station what the disturbance was and followed the others up Kessler's alley to Liberty Street. Manuel said he glanced at Tessie Morgan's windows as he passed and saw no light there. Said about two dozen people were in back of feed store and milling around Sheppard's car. Said he remained only short time because firemen ordered him out into the square. Said that all the people were congregated in the north end at the entrance of Liberty Street, and by the time Sergeant Boyle arrived there were about five hundred people crowded in front of Johnson's feed store and across the end of Liberty Street. Said he did not notice bank building. Said he knew Frederick Thorne by sight but did not see him at any time Thursday night.

Patrick J. and Margaret Morgan, 171 Mill Street. P.J. employed Kendall-Sudwich mill as stationary engineer. Tessie one of two children: other, son, Patrick Jr., employed in tool plant in Hartford. Son was at home and offered co-operation refused by parents. Son making funeral arrangements with Elmdale mortuary. Unable to furnish much information as had not seen sister in nearly a year. He said trouble with family had started when Tessie won dining-room suite as award in beauty contest sponsored by mill; she wanted to set up her own establishment right away. No clothing or other personal effects in Mill Street house. Named Annie Clayton as high school chum who might be able to give further information.

Annie Clayton, 14 River Street. Employed in Kendall mill as loom operator. Had seen little of Tessie after her elevation to secretary. Said success had gone to Tessie's head. Only information of value: it was Tessie who had received the notification from the War Department that Bill Stanczyk was missing in action. And Tessie kept a diary. Note: no close personal friends.

(*At least,* Dickerson told himself, *we seem to have solved the mystery of Miss Morgan's dining-room furniture.*)

More from Sergeant Boyle: Deliah Birdwell, Heaths' maid; sleeps in; employed in New Haven about a year ago. Deliah Birdwell stated that on Thursday night Mrs. Heath permitted her to go to the movies, and after stacking the dishes to dry, she left the house at about a quarter before eight. At that time Heath had gone out, and Mrs. Heath was sitting in the living-room, reading. Miss Birdwell returned from movies at quarter to ten, at which time both Mr. and Mrs. Heath were in living-room engaged in earnest conversation. She said they were still there when she went to bed about ten minutes later.

Deliah said that on following morning (Friday), she inspected both Mr. and Mrs. Heath's closets to see if any clothes needed cleaning or pressing and found none. She said further that no clothes were missing. On direction question, she admitted Mrs. Heath had acted upset during the evening, but thought it might be because of her father's illness.

Henry Heath: Mr. Heath stated that he had visited Ford Sheppard's residence, arriving at a little after seven-thirty and departing at shortly after eight-thirty, to discuss recasting the mortgage on his house and also to negotiate an additional loan. Heath stated that he and Sheppard had reached complete agreement on both matters and that Sheppard had the money (twenty thousand dollars) at the house. Heath said, however, that the form of the note was objectionable to him, Sheppard had handed him the money without demanding a receipt, and that he would prepare the note in the desired form for his signature the following day.

Heath said that on returning to his house he discovered that he had left his gloves at the Sheppard residence and so he immediately returned. He said that the door was unlocked and he admitted himself and went directly to the study where the conference had taken place, and there he picked up his gloves and departed. Heath said that he could hear the maids talking in the kitchen, and that Sheppard was at that time apparently taking a shower because he could hear the sound of water and whistling in the upper parts of the house.

Heath said that it was a little before nine when he returned to his home and that Mrs. Heath was there. He said they sat down and had a long talk, mostly about the illness of Mrs. Heath's father. He said they retired at about quarter-past ten.

Prudence Heath: Supported statements made by husband and Deliah Birdwell. Said she did not leave the house except for a few minutes around eight o'clock when she walked downtown to post a letter. She emphatically denied having been anywhere near Tessie Morgan's apartment.

Note: No other witness found to corroborate statement from Manuel Zella that Mrs. Heath visited Morgan's apartment Thursday night.

Dickerson leaned back, staring at the wall. Would there be any particular point in Zella lying about having seen Mrs. Heath? If he had merely wanted to invent someone to protect Ben Sutts, why would he pick Mrs. Heath? And she, certainly, in the light of later events, would hardly want to admit of a visit to Miss Morgan, no matter how innocent that visit might have been.

And another fact stood out in the reports. If it was to be assumed that the scarecrow was not Cotton Kendall but actually Bill Stanczyk, and it was to be believed that Stanczyk had been in a Boston hospital on Wednesday night; and if it could be accepted as fact that the Stanczyk was suffering from total amnesia, then who was the person who had stood behind Frederick Thorne's screen? Had there been such a person? If so, where had he come by the knowledge that had so convinced Thorne into accepting him, sight unseen, as Cotton Kendall?

Had it been DeSylvia? DeSylvia's time

on Wednesday night was unaccounted for. But where would DeSylvia get the information necessary to fool Thorne? As the scarecrow's guardian on the trip from San Diego, he would have been in charge of Cotton Kendall's effects. Those effects could well have included letters from Frederick Thorne, and the letters could have contained all that DeSylvia needed.

Yet, for what purpose? Why should DeSylvia suspect that his charge was anyone other than Cotton Kendall?

Could it have been Marion, Cotton's wife, who had stood behind that screen? She wouldn't need any letters; to win Thorne's confidence she wouldn't need any more information than she already had as Cotton's wife. Yet why would Marion Kendall resort to hiding behind a screen to obtain a portrait when all she had to do was state her purpose and make the request? And by her own admission, she had been with Ford Sheppard that night, trying without any success to tell him that her husband had returned.

What would Marion Kendall have to gain by such a course?

Or could the person have been Prudence Heath? Cotton's half-sister wouldn't have needed any coaching. But why? There was no single shred of evidence which would tend to show that she knew her half-brother to be no longer missing, even at the present time. That fact was a well-guarded secret being closely held between the old man, Cotton's wife, DeSylvia, Matthew Swayle, M.D., and Julian Martens.

And of all those people, only Martens knew that the scarecrow was not Cotton Kendall!

Dickerson's eyes abruptly lost their introspective stare. From the noise on the front porch, and from the noiseless entrance of Mrs. Boyle to the kitchen, it appeared that the lord and master was returning to his house and that supper, long overdue, was in the works.

Dickerson turned to Postman Boyle, whose comfortable snooze the swift developments had disturbed, and asked, 'Is there a library in this town, and if so, is it open now?'

'A library? Yes, sir. It's on School Street, near Main. About three blocks from the post office. Let's see, today's Saturday and it's half-past six. I believe the library's open 'til eight.'

'Good.' As Dickerson stood up, he was confronted by Sergeant Boyle. The sergeant acted as if he were tired, and his immediate announcement that he was hungry brought with it a swift, suspicious glance at the obdurate back of the woman who was coaxing miracles from the kitchen range.

'Perry Thompson relieved me,' Boyle answered in response to Dickerson's question. 'Perry ate an hour ago. But I don't know about Kohler. I don't know what we're going to do about feeding him.'

'Kohler's used to it,' Dickerson said. 'There's just one more job I want you to do.'

Boyle had rolled back his sleeves and was busy with soap at the kitchen sink. 'Right away?' he asked anxiously.

'No. After you've had your supper, you are to visit the local stationery stores. We want to know if Tessie Morgan had purchased a diary; since the month is now March, it would not have been more than

three months ago, and should be remembered. If possible, we want a duplicate of
that diary; if they have none in stock, they
might recall having sold a similar one to
another person — '

There was another loud commotion at
the front door, followed by heavy, hurry-
ing footsteps in the hall. It was Constable
Westcott, considerably out of breath.

'I just seen Swayle,' Westcott gasped.
'Old man Kendall's had another heart
attack. They took him t' th' hospital. He's
dyin'. They got his daughter, Prue, all
right, but when they tried to reach his
daughter-in-law at th' Tolberts, Mrs.
Tolbert said she ain't seen her since
half-past four. Said she rode off with
some stranger, a nice-looking white-
haired man — car had Massachusetts
plates.'

10

At five minutes past eight, Miss Spence, the librarian, wondered if the large gentleman in the Oxford grey overcoat was ever going to leave. He had been paging through the newspaper files for more than an hour and a half and had made her go twice to the upstairs store-room for an additional supply of *The Boston Globe*. At present, he was solemnly turning the pages of the bound volume for the first quarter of nineteen thirty-eight.

Not that he was causing any trouble. He was really most polite, and he was quite handsome too, with his flashing grey eyes and the distinguished touch of silver at his temples.

He had stopped; perhaps he had at last found whatever it was that he was looking for. False alarm. He began, with solemn precision, to turn the pages again.

See here, Mr. Moustache. This library closes at eight!

Distinguished or not, trouble or no, it was now fifteen minutes past closing time and he would simply *have* to leave. Miss Spence raised her small and rather plump body to determined erectness and stalked forth from the fortress of her desk.

'I am very sorry,' she said with firmness, 'but I have to close the library now.'

What next occurred, according to Miss Spence, she had never been quite able to fully comprehend. She wasn't, she later told friends, sure if he had hypnotized her or not; she did know she was totally unable to recall any single word he had spoken. But he had said *something*. Whatever it was, it was sufficient to make her retire in utter defeat. And so, on the Saturday night of March twenty-third, the Sudwich library remained open until the historic and unprecedented hour of a quarter to nine.

At twenty minutes before nine, Miss Spence recounted, the large man's fist had struck the periodical table with a mighty crash. She had seen that the large gentleman was scribbling madly in a small black notebook. And when she had risen to ask him if he was *quite* through, he had been dashing towards her desk.

'He,' Miss Spence said, 'was completely mad. He actually *kissed* me!'

Great though the shock of that might have been, she retained enough native curiosity to seek the cause of the outburst. And she found it on the sporting page of a Boston newspaper for February 12, 1937. A very erratic check mark in ink appeared beside a double-column box heading: 'SMITH PARRIES AND THRUSTS FOIL WELLESLEY HOPES.'

Miss Spence could not see, really, anything to get excited about.

★　★　★

When Dickerson crossed the porch of the Boyle house and entered the hall, he found the elder Boyle at the telephone. The postman's head revolved, and his fierce blue eyes showed intense relief.

'Here he is now,' the postman said. 'Hold on a minute — it's for you, Lieutenant.'

Dickerson took over. 'This is Connelly,'

his unmistakable voice said. 'Martens hasn't come back yet, and now DeSylvia's slipped out on me. What'll I do?'

'Did you check with the ticket windows?'

'Yeah. Nothing there. If this guy Cotton Kendall went to Sudwich on a train, he paid cash fare to the conductor. DeSylvia bought a New Haven round trip Thursday — I found that out by — '

'I don't care how you found out. What about Martens?'

'Listen, he has a car and a physician's gas ration book. Why should he worry about trains?'

'You're sure he hasn't returned yet?'

'Sure I'm sure. The people at the hospital are worried. He said he'd be back by five o'clock, but he hasn't been there and he hasn't been home.'

'All right. Keep going. This thing will have to break soon.'

Dickerson had no chance to hang up before the telephone gave a burring rattle.

This time it was Kohler. 'I'm in Thorne's studio,' Kohler's laconic voice said. 'He's careless as hell — leaves

318

everything unlocked. I've been in and out a dozen times. A train just went zooming by here a few minutes ago, and then the phone rang. Right afterwards, Thorne came out and climbed in his bus and took off. I just saw his tail-light as he turned over the bridge — think he might have gone to the station.'

Dickerson's heart began to miss beats. 'Tail him over there. Cross the railway bridge. If I'm not there yet, wait for me. And don't take any chances.'

'Don't worry about Kohler.'

Dickerson didn't even have a chance to take the receiver from his ear. 'Mr. Dickerson! Don't hang up!' It was Jennie, and she was excited. 'Say, I've been listening in — Mr. Thorne's call did come from the station, and it was the same voice that called him Thursday night. And right afterwards, the same voice called the Tolberts' house. I was so busy getting the other call through to you I didn't have a chance to listen on that one. But whoever he was, he told Thorne to meet him because he had just come in on the train. But you know what? That train didn't stop!'

'Good heavens!' Dickerson shouted.

And then he was racing down the hall. 'Boyle! We've got to stop them! *Boyle!*'

Sergeant Boyle appeared at the head of the stairs. The seeds of sleep were still in his eyes, and he had no shoes on, but he did not hesitate. He came bounding down the stairs, and without even stopping to pick up his hat, plunged out into the night in the direction Dickerson had gone.

★　★　★

The thin moon was obscured by clouds, and the warehouses and their flanking lumber piles were ghostly silhouettes against the dark sky as the Buick flashed quietly down the deserted street.

Boyle, at the wheel, was neither wasting time nor taking chances. Straight down the centre he drove, increasing speed between intersections, holding his foot in readiness at the brake as street openings appeared. But Boyle was also thinking of what a strange and unpredictable man this Dickerson was. Less than three hours ago, when Constable Westcott had arrived with the news about old man Kendall and the startling information that Marion Kendall had apparently been abducted by Martens, Dickerson hadn't turned a hair. He had calmly walked to the telephone, called Boston and issued a few crisp orders, and then had turned about to remind Boyle about the diary. And then he had marched off to the library.

The Buick slowed as Boyle's firm hand negotiated a swing left. They were running parallel to and a block distant from the railway right-of-way. The station was in sight across the intervening vacant land, and the signal lights in the tower beyond it showed green. They were fast approaching the cross street that led directly to the station, and the Buick's headlights threw the triangular billboard at the corner into bold relief.

Dickerson gripped Boyle's arm. 'Easy, now,' he said tersely. 'Go slow past those signboards.'

Boyle nodded and transferred the pressure of his foot from accelerator to brake. As they passed the signboards and swung right, Dickerson let out a little grunt of satisfaction. His head turned. 'Did you see it?' he asked.

Boyle nodded. He had seen the car parked behind the billboards; had seen and recognized that it bore a Massachusetts licence plate.

'Cut your lights!'

Boyle cut them, but not until they had picked out Thorne's battered station wagon, standing at an angle in the parking yard. And Thorne himself, standing hesitant on the platform at the head of the wooden steps.

Against the black bulk of the Kendall-Sudwich mills, the small brick waiting room was an almost indistinguishable blur. At Dickerson's whispered request, Boyle stopped and pulled to the side of the road just before the entrance to the parking yard.

Dickerson's hand was on his arm again. 'There's a car coming,' he said. 'We'll wait.'

Straight up the street a small coupé came, travelling fast. It passed them too swiftly to make possible identification of the occupant, but Boyle saw that it was a woman. The coupé bounced over the gutter and into the parking yard and slid to a stop beside Thorne's station wagon.

'Now,' Dickerson said tersely, 'take your flashlight and go up to the left of the station. Stay on the ground at the corner of the platform. Post yourself where you can watch both platform and street. I'll go up on the right. If I shout, come running. Quick, now!'

They quit the car, and Boyle moved at a run that quickly slowed to a limping trot as loose pebbles sent thrusts of pain up through his thinly stockinged feet. The ground was rough and cold, and as Boyle headed for what looked like the biggest assignment of his life, he realized in sudden desperation how ill prepared he was. He had no hat, he had no shoes, and worst of all his pistol was blissfully hanging from its holster at the head of his bed.

Boyle groaned, as much from despair at his own stupidity as at the agony of his feet. He reached the platform and moved along it, facing the tracks. *Stay on the ground*, Dickerson *had said, and post yourself where you can watch*. Boyle found his view of the platform blocked by pulled-up express trucks, and he backed away.

The night was still, the cold-stillness of a March night in New England. Far down the curving tracks, beyond the turnbridge and on the spit of land that made the dunes, an eastbound freight grunted against its load. The locomotive's fire door was open, casting a red glow against the sky, and its headlight made a black and spidery silhouette of the turnbridge. The bridge was closed, and the shining green of a block signal pencilled through.

So near that its report was deafening, a shot sounded.

Boyle uttered a cry and scrambled to the platform, clutching his flashlight. Aided by its light, he dodged an express truck and came around the protruding edge of the waiting room. And then in utter amazement he stopped.

The circle of light brought into vivid outline a tableau. He saw Dickerson, kneeling, supporting on his arm the burnished auburn head of Marion Kendall. She was lying on her side, on the wooden platform, her face white and distorted in pain.

Beyond her stood another woman whom Boyle did not recognize at once because she was holding the back of her hand against her mouth. But then she took a slow step forward, and he saw that she was Mrs. Tolbert. And there, in the centre of all of it, was Fred Thorne.

Thorne was hunched over, and straightening slowly. Thorne's eyes were blinking owlishly in a vapidly blank face. His left arm was at a stiff angle from his body, and in his bony left hand dangled a pistol.

Boyle became rigid. 'Give me that gun!' he shouted.

Thorne turned slowly, staring owlishly at the dazzling circle of light. Hesitantly his hand moved out.

Dickerson glanced up, his face pale and stern. 'Boyle!' he cried sharply. 'Don't touch that pistol!'

'But — '

'Thorne, drop the thing to the platform. *Drop it, I say!*'

Almost reluctantly, Thorne stooped and dropped the pistol to the worn wood planking.

Mrs. Tolbert's hand dropped from her

mouth. 'He killed her!' she cried hysterically. 'I saw him! I wasn't three feet away. Oh, my poor darling! Speak to me — say something to me.'

Dickerson fixed Mrs. Tolbert with a savage eye and said, '*Shut up!*'

Mrs. Tolbert began to weep, and Boyle bristled. This thing didn't make sense. Here was Marion Kendall, who had been shot. And here was Fred Thorne, who might have killed heaven alone knew how many people, caught this time red-handed. He was holding the pistol, and the pistol had been in his left hand.

Yet there knelt Dickerson, calmly telling Thorne to drop the pistol, and savagely telling Mrs. Tolbert to *shut up*!

Dickerson said, 'Mrs. Kendall hasn't been killed. She's been shot in the fleshy part of the thigh. I suggest that you, Mrs. Tolbert, control yourself long enough to call an ambulance.' And then Dickerson turned his head and bellowed, '*Kohler!*'

A running shadow emerged from the edge of darkness along the right-of-way. 'Yeah, Joe?' Kohler's panting voice came.

'Martens, the party that called on

Thorne this afternoon; he's around here somewhere. Find him!'

Kohler started, but another shadow had already detached itself from the deep gloom of the eastbound platform, the width of two tracks away. 'I shall be there immediately!' the surgeon's voice rang above the noise of the approaching freight. 'But I suggest that someone call the ambulance at once. I have nothing with me but my hands.'

The nearing freight had struck the straight stretch now, and the space between the east- and westbound platforms was charged with the glare of the locomotive's headlight. The surgeon's passage over the tracks prompted the locomotive to a shrill protesting whistle which did not serve to accelerate his unhurried pace, and as he mounted to the platform Kohler was but a step behind.

Sergeant Boyle was badly confused, but it was he who finally had to call the ambulance after borrowing a nickel from Dickerson. Call completed, he turned his attention to the platform again. He saw that Frederick Thorne hadn't moved, but that Martens had replaced Dickerson at

Marion Kendall's side. Dickerson was standing by Mrs. Tolbert, her weeping subsiding to sniffles. And Kohler was sagging, apparently indifferent and half-asleep against the waiting room door.

Martens had pulled up Marion Kendall's dress and his thumb had found a pressure point, stopping the flow of blood. The wound looked nasty, and Boyle could see that the least inconvenience Marion Kendall would suffer would be a long time in bed.

Boyle could see a great deal more, too; he blushed and turned his face away.

A hissing, roaring rumble filled the night as the freight came through, sweeping past the group on the platform. At his post against the door, Kohler moved slightly, and a beam of light leaped from his indifferent hand to cut diagonally across the grave face of Julian Martens and rest on the stooped, owlishly blinking Frederic Thorne.

Dickerson pulled away from Mrs. Tolbert and walked over to where the pistol lay. The large man squatted down, drew a handkerchief from his pocket, and carefully picked up the pistol, bundling it in his overcoat pocket. Then he stood and came directly to Boyle.

He put his mouth to Boyle's ear and asked, 'Were you able to locate a diary?'

Boyle waited for a flat wheel to go thumping by. 'It's in the car,' he said. 'Tessie had bought one in Sanford's drug store, and Sanford had sold one just like it to Swayle. I borrowed Swayle's, but he wants it back. He keeps his appointments in it.'

Dickerson squeezed Boyle's elbow. 'Good! Now, when we leave I want you to stay behind. First, satisfy yourself that there's no one else hanging around here. Then get under the platform and work your light. I think you'll find something of interest not far from the edge. Dickerson grinned. 'After that, stop by your house and get your shoes and hat before you join us at the hospital.'

★　★　★

When they reached the hospital they found that Swayle had his hands full with old man Kendall, but there was a younger man, a Dr. Leonard, who had just finished an emergency appendectomy, now working on Marion Kendall. And while an overworked nurse was preparing the young woman, Dr. Leonard carefully explained to Dickerson just what he would do. He would give her a shot of tetanus serum and before probing the wound would administer a spinal anaesthetic so that if Dickerson wished to question her later, he could do so with perfect safety. The pellet had apparently gone straight through. There was no reason why, he said, she couldn't be up and around in a few days.

Leonard arranged for them to wait in the doctor's sitting room, and so it was here, augmented by a distraught and reluctant Henry Heath, that they arranged themselves.

Mrs. Tolbert, at Marion Kendall's request, had been permitted to accompany her into the operating-room, and so it was an all-male gathering that remained. Frederick Thorne, pale, worn and confused, sat in a low-backed rocker in a corner of bookshelves. At his left, stiff and solemn, was Julian Martens, his no-longer twinkling eyes watching Dickerson's every move.

Dickerson faced these two, and at his right Henry Heath shook and perspired in a straight-backed maple chair. Completing the group was Kohler, stretched on a mohair couch, soulfully chewing on a sandwich he had managed to wangle from a nurse.

Dickerson removed the handkerchief-wrapped pistol from his pocket and held it out towards Thorne. 'Is this your pistol?' he demanded.

Thorne reached into his jacket pocket and brought out a small snub-nosed revolver which he indifferently tossed to Dickerson's lap. 'This is mine,' his voice boomed. 'Take the damned thing. I'm tired of toting it around. I started carrying it to protect myself, but it looks like what I need is a lawyer.'

'It wouldn't hurt you to have one,' Dickerson agreed. 'And you'd better get a good one. This, then, is not your pistol?'

'No. Why would I want two?'

Dickerson shrugged. Carefully, he broke the pistol on the handkerchief, examined the cylinder breech, and then passed it around, holding it before the eyes of each of the others.

'I want you to notice this,' he said calmly. 'You saw me pick up this pistol on the station platform and wrap it in the handkerchief. That is, all of you but Mr. Heath. I have not been out of your sight since, and so you know that not until now have I broken the breech of this pistol. All right, what do see?'

'A single cartridge only,' Martens answered promptly.

Dickerson nodded, closed the pistol, rewrapped it and returned it to his pocket. Breaking Thorne's pistol, he repeated the performance, showed them that it was fully loaded, removed the cartridges to show that none of them had been fired, and without reloading the pistol stuffed it in his other pocket.

'Now, Mr. Thorne,' he said briskly, 'I shall ask you some questions.'

Henry Heath leaned forward anxiously. 'Couldn't you start with me first? I really ought to get back to my wife. She — her father is dying.'

With faint irony, Dickerson said, 'I

doubt that your presence would materially assist your father-in-law's state of health or mind. I will have to ask you to remain here. Now, Mr. Thorne, on Wednesday evening you had a visitor to whom you entrusted a pastel portrait, and on Thursday evening you received a telephone call. We believe that we know who it was that made the call, but we want to know what it was about.'

Thorne's eyes burned briefly. 'And if I do not choose to tell you?'

Dickerson shrugged. 'That is your prerogative, but you're being foolish. Perhaps I can guess the nature of that call. Someone requested you to meet him in front of the bank building at, say, ten o'clock. The someone was insistent and quite distressed, and you agreed. You had quite a bit of time on your hands, so you decided to take care of another matter first. You armed yourself and went in search of Ford Sheppard. You visited his house and learned he was not there, and then you visited the Dunes Club and learned he had just left. So, your time being used up, you proceeded to keep your appointment in Sudwich Square.'

Thorne's knuckles were white against the arm of the chair. 'So you beat it out of him, did you?' His voice was resonant with bitterness. 'You sat his poor, tired, broken body in a chair and worked on him with your tricks. You rotten swine!'

'Mr. Thorne, you have too much imagination,' Dickerson said evenly. 'That is your one great weakness. Except for a few of us 'rotten swine', you might very well be talking to your lawyer behind bars instead of to us in this pleasant room. So you kept your appointment, and at precisely ten o'clock you heard the sound of a shot. You left your car and proceeded up the alley between the bank and the feed store, crossed over to the platform at the rear of the feed store, and there stopped because you saw Perry Thompson coming down the centre of the street. You then returned to your car and were just entering it when Constable Westcott came running across the square. You accompanied Westcott into Liberty Street and there saw the body of Ford Sheppard in his Packard coupé. You formed your own conclusions, proceeded at Westcott's behest to the fire station where you summoned a guard, and then you went home.'

Dickerson paused, his face stern. 'Answer me!' he said sharply. 'Is that correct?'

'Oh, Judas Priest — yes! You seem to know every damned thing I do!'

'And tonight the same voice called you and asked you to come to the railway station, and you obeyed. Now, what happened from the moment you stepped on that platform?'

Thorne's white, drawn face was troubled. 'I'm not exactly sure . . . I proceeded along the platform to where I thought I saw a shadowy figure — '

There was an interruption. Sergeant Boyle came in quickly closed the door. Boyle was fully dressed and his pistol was strapped on. He was carrying a long, slender package in his hands and he nodded at Dickerson before he went over to sit down near Kohler.

'Got it,' Boyle said.

' — and I stopped,' Thorne resumed his story. 'Suddenly, almost in front of my face, there was a flash and a *bang*! Naturally I was stunned. The next thing I knew I heard a woman, Tolbert, screaming; and then a flashlight was turned in my face, and there I was with a pistol in my hand.' He halted lamely. 'That's the way it was.'

Dickerson nodded. 'All right. Now, Dr. Martens, we come to you.'

The surgeon's look of gravity had been replaced by one of interest, and the twinkle had returned to his eyes, along with admiration. 'I am quite ready,' he said.

They were all of them leaning forward. Heath had stopped his fidgeting and was watching with eyes as bright as a child's before a window full of toys. They hadn't noticed it before, but now they saw that Dickerson was holding a small red-leather bound book, riffling the pages with apparent unconcern.

Dickerson said, 'I suppose, Martens, that you realize what an unholy spot you've put yourself in?'

The surgeon exhaled. 'I most assuredly do, Lieutenant. I am rapidly losing interest in my formerly number one hobby. As you know, I was convinced that Mrs. Kendall was the victim of a conspiracy, so after I left you I went directly to the house, the Tolbert residence where she was staying. I asked Mrs. Kendall if she would care to return to Boston with me, and she said no, that she had heard from DeSylvia and that everything was taken care of. She then asked me, quite naturally, why I had concealed from her the fact that her husband was in my hospital.'

Martens spread his hands. 'I admit that I acted most foolishly in so doing. I offered her my humble apologies and my sincere services. She graciously accepted the first, but for the second she said the only service I could perform at the moment was to drive her in town because she wished to visit a Mrs. Sturgis, an old family retainer. I readily agreed; she entered my car and we drove to a small white house in the residential section on the hill. Both Mrs. Sturgis and Mrs. Kendall insisted that I remain for tea, so I did. I left these two delightful ladies at approximately a quarter to six.'

Martens paused, and the twinkle faded

from his eyes. 'And now, Lieutenant,' he said, 'comes the part — er — which may be difficult to explain ... maybe I too should first consult my lawyer. However, having been permitted to share certain aspects of the case with you, and having had the opportunity to glance over your notes in the Boyle kitchen while you were receiving a telephone call from Boston, I had become quite convinced that Marion Kendall's life was in danger. I therefore appointed to myself the task of guarding her. I drove my car from the Sturgis house, parked it at the nearest convenient spot, and returned to set up my vigil. I satisfied myself that she was still in the house because I saw her as she passed a window.

'This business of shadowing being new to me, I found interesting. Shortly after eight o'clock, Mrs. Kendall came out and proceeded to walk down to the centre of town. I followed at a discreet distance. When we entered Liberty Street from Mizzen Hill Road I was a half-block behind. I saw her clearly outlined in the lights from the square. And then, quite inexplicably, I lost her.

'Thinking she might have entered a store, I made as thorough a search of the vicinity as discretion would permit, but to no avail. I was at a loss. Had she got into a waiting car? I hoped not, for that was one of the things I feared.'

The surgeon bent forward. 'At that point I very nearly went on to the Boyle residence, to lay this latest puzzle before you. But I was reluctant, because I had caused you enough annoyance. Then I recalled your notes, and the thought occurred to me that in all of the things that had happened in Sudwich, nearly every one had had its point of origin at the pay telephone of the railway station. Immediately I retrieved my car, drove to the station, parked it out of sight, and repaired to the eastbound platform to wait.'

Martens gave a long sigh. 'I know it sounds awful, but that's the way it was.'

Dickerson had returned the diary to his pocket, and the light of amusement that had at brief times during Martens' recital rested in his eyes was gone. Abruptly he turned and faced Henry Heath.

'Now, Mr. Heath, I will ask you to tell me the terms of your father-in-law's will. I believe you were well acquainted with them.'

The fat little man's tongue stuck to the roof of his mouth with a ludicrous clucking sound. 'Don't — don't you think that question is just a bit uncalled for?'

'No more uncalled for than your actions have been.'

Perspiration stood out on Heath's neck. 'Well, if Cotton were to die first, my wife would get the bulk of the estate. That's the last one I know of. He's changed it several times.'

'Then why were you conspiring with Sheppard to gain control of the mill?'

'Say, look here — '

'Come off it, Heath,' Dickerson said disgustedly. 'The least I can do to you right now is send you to jail for the misappropriation of Sheppard's twenty thousand dollars. You were manager of the mill and you were married to the owner's daughter. What in the name of heaven were you thinking of?'

340

Heath's round face was very red. 'Well, what with Cotton's status the way it was, and with the old man so sick, I was afraid we might be — '

There was a swift, sharp knock at the door. It opened almost at once to admit a nurse whose tired eyes clashed with the freshness of her starched uniform. She looked about quickly, settled on Henry Heath and said, 'Would you step to the door a moment, please?'

Heath arose hastily and went out. There was a drone of conversation, only a few words, behind the closed door.

Heath reappeared. His flabby face was now a slightly bilious yellow. His eyes, fixed on Dickerson, held pleading. 'Sir,' he asked in a muffled voice, 'would it be all right if — if I go now? My wife needs me. Mr. Kendall just died.'

Dickerson stood, and there was no irony in him as he replied. 'It will be quite all right, Mr. Heath. I'm sorry to hear it. I doubt if we'll be bothering you again.'

★　★　★

'You may see her now,' the nurse said.

Dickerson followed her down the long hall, climbed stairs, and entered the room which the nurse, with a nod, indicated. She left him there, and before he had closed the door she was already off on her endless rounds.

Marion Kendall lay with closed eyes, as pale as the linen about her, and her outstretched hand held the hand of Mrs. Tolbert, who was seated at her bedside. Young Doctor Leonard was standing by, his circular mirror still attached to his head, drawing off long rubber gloves.

'You may question her now if you wish,' Leonard said. 'But don't make it too long. She's suffering a bit from shock.'

'I have no desire to question her,' Dickerson said quietly. 'The man who might want to is Frederick Thorne. He might want to ask why she so deliberately and persistently tried to frame him into the electric chair. But I believe I can give him his answer.'

Mrs. Tolbert gasped. But beyond a slight flush that appeared in her face, Marion

Kendall neither opened her eyes nor gave other evidence that she had heard.

Young Dr. Leonard's features were vacant with surprise. 'She is a consummate actress, that one,' Dickerson told him, but there was no admiration in his voice. 'She fooled Thorne into thinking that she was her husband. And she fooled DeSylvia into thinking that the scarecrow, Stanczyk, was Cotton Kendall. She almost fooled Postman Boyle, too, but most of all she fooled herself.'

Mrs. Tolbert had started to rise. 'If this is a form of the third degree,' she said in a strangled voice, 'I'm sure that Marion's lawyers will have something to say to you. I was directly behind Frederick Thorne on the station platform. I saw him shoot her!'

'I compliment you on your eyesight, Mrs. Tolbert. I was directly behind *you*, and I couldn't even distinguish the colour of your coat. Hasn't it occurred to you why you were summoned to that out-of-the-way place at that time of night?'

Mrs. Tolbert replied, stiffly, 'Certainly. I came to pick Marion up. She called me and asked me to.'

Dickerson turned to Leonard, who was now glancing, with hardness and a little speculation, at the still figure on the bed.

'You saw the wound. Tell me, what course did the bullet take?'

'The course was slanting, downward and to the left.'

'And at what range had the bullet been fired?'

'Very close. Not above fifteen inches.'

Dickerson looked at Mrs. Tolbert now. 'Your friend was very clever,' he said, 'but she made two costly mistakes. The first was in the very beginning, when she was standing behind the screen in Thorne's studio. She had come there for the sole purpose of convincing him that her husband was alive; DeSylvia was in Sudwich, waiting for her, wanting some word to take back to the suspicious Martens; and as she talked she faced the pastel portrait of her husband. Here was something that would convince anyone; she added it to her plan with the same swift dexterity that she had later employed in seizing an opportune weapon to kill Tessie Morgan. But she erred sadly; she had never noticed the size and shape of the scarecrow's ears — they are a feature most of us take little notice of; but they are the most characteristic and least susceptible to change.

'Her second great mistake was tonight. She had held the pistol in her left hand when she killed Ford Sheppard because she wanted us to believe it was Thorne who had killed him; that was why she brought Thorne to the square with the faked telephone call. And so tonight, when she became suspicious of Martens and felt that she must divert suspicion from herself, again the faked telephone call. Only this time she must have a witness, someone whose testimony would be believed. That, Mrs. Tolbert, is why you were summoned to pick her up.

'I have said that she made this second mistake, and it was here that she made it. She wanted to frame Thorne to a finish; he was to be caught seemingly in the act of shooting her. But willing as she was to take chances with other people's lives, she would not risk her own; she shot herself in the fleshy part of the thigh, where the bullet would do the least possible damage — forgetting that a man who could shoot and kill Sheppard with one shot at twenty inches could hardly go so wide of his target at fifteen.'

Marion Kendall's eyes were no longer closed. They were open now and staring with intent hatred.

'I will fight you,' she said in her low, husky voice, 'through every court in the land!'

Dickerson looked at her. There was sadness, and a bit of wistfulness, in his glance. 'You will gain a little time,' he said, 'but that is all.'

★ ★ ★

Dickerson stepped to the exact centre of the faded green carpet, stiffened to attention and said, 'Yes, Commissioner?'

The commissioner looked up from the reports he was reading, scowled, waved a hand as large and hairy as a coconut and said, 'Sit down!'

Dickerson found a chair. 'Is there something wrong?' he asked anxiously.

'Wrong?' the commissioner bellowed. 'I should say there is! My gosh, you can't go around accusing prominent people of murder! I told you this was no two-bit shooting affray. That woman's going to fight, and when she's through we'll be the whipping boys of New England! Have you lost your *mind?*'

'No, sir. I just haven't had time to make my full report.'

'You'll make it, now, to me. And I'm warning you, it better be good!'

So Dickerson started. He told how DeSylvia had brought the scarecrow to the Kendall house, how of all the household only Marion had seen him, and how, up until then, she had thought her husband was missing in action.

'You see, sir,' Dickerson said anxiously, 'so long as Cotton was missing, his wife was safe. By safe, I mean safe in the sense of financial security. The desire for wealth and luxury had been the motivating force in her entire life. When her father-in-law eventually discovered this, after practically shanghaiing his son into marriage with her, he changed his will so that if his son should die before he did, his entire estate would go to his daughter Prudence Heath.

'You can readily see Marion's position. If Cotton were declared dead, she would be kicked out without a dime except for the few bonds her father had left her, and the income from them hadn't been enough to support her house.'

The commissioner snorted. 'Call that a motive? Any wet-eared correspondence-school lawyer could rip that to shreds by merely pointing to the fact that Sheppard wanted to marry her, and Sheppard was rich!'

Dickerson reddened. 'Begging your pardon, sir, but Sheppard was not as rich as people thought, and she was in an excellent position to know through her brother-in-law, Harold Finch, the bank cashier. And the stakes in the Kendall game were better than a million dollars.'

The commissioner relaxed a little. 'A million, huh?'

'Yes, sir. When Marion saw the scarecrow she knew, of course, that he was not Cotton Kendall. She was in a terrible spot. If the old man should get to see him, the game would end right there. So she inveigled DeSylvia into taking him on to Boston to the great plastic surgeon, Martens. It had been almost eight years since Martens had known Cotton in Sudwich, and then only casually, and the hulk of a man who had come back was so changed there wasn't much danger of his being identified as someone else. And anyway, all she wanted to do was get him covered with bandages until the old man conveniently died; after that she'd be in control of the million and she didn't care. And the old man was very sick; at the most it was a question of few months.'

The commissioner turned back to the reports. He read for awhile, then looked up at Dickerson.

'So she slapped a green felt hat on his head and sent him downtown while DeSylvia wasn't looking, and then 'discovered' that he'd wandered off?'

'Yes, sir. Her purpose was to establish his presence, to be seen with him just long enough for people to start asking questions. Unfortunately he ran into the one person in the world she least wanted him to see — Tessie Morgan. Marion learned this fact from a fellow passenger on the Boston train Thursday afternoon, a very vicious gossip by the name of Reba Johnson. And so Marion had to return to Sudwich and remove Tessie, the only person left in Sudwich who would know Bill Stanczyk well enough to identify him — just as she had to remove Ford Sheppard because he had threatened to start an investigation which could result only in determining that Cotton Kendall was dead.

'We can prove premeditation because we can show that Marion stole Sheppard's pistol from the glove compartment of his car at some time prior to Thursday night; probably on Wednesday night when she had her last date with him. Her Boston trip, then, was to establish an alibi, and she did it quite cleverly by enlisting the aid of a friend, Alice Wentworth, to call hotels and hospitals far into the night, asking for Cotton Kendall or Carlos DeSylvia. Having set up all this clamour, she quietly slipped down to South Station, inconspicuously boarded the same train that Reba

Johnson and her daughter Julie were returning on, and landed in Sudwich at five minutes past nine — Incidentally, that Sudwich station is darker than the inside of a cow.

'Marion immediately called Thorne, using the disguised voice that had fooled him before, and told him to be in front of the bank at ten. She then went straight to Tessie Morgan's apartment.

'She could not have descended on Miss Morgan at a more opportune moment. Tessie had had a fight with Ben Sutts and was scared to death of him. She'd had a fight with Heath on the previous morning, and in the course of that fight had seen someone who gave her the not impossible idea that Bill Stanczyk had come home to kill her. And less than a half-hour before, she had suffered a very embarrassing tongue lashing from Prudence Heath.

'For purposes of defence, Tessie had borrowed a sword-cane from Frederick Thorne; Tessie showed it to Marion, and there the method, which was quieter and therefore safer than the pistol she had in her bag, sprang into full bloom.'

Dickerson paused. 'I can see the scene very clearly, sir,' he said. 'Marion takes the sword from Tessie, balances it and says, 'Look, my dear. I'll teach you how to use this. Then you can really defend yourself. I was on the fencing team at Smith; we had an excellent team. We defeated Wellesley that year. Now you stand over there as if you were about to attack me. Just as if I were you and you were Ben Sutts. Now, you see, this is the first position; I cry 'On guard!' And this is *prime*, and this *tierce*.' And with *tierce* she let her have it. Tessie Morgan swayed, and fell forward, full on the sword —

'Marion then lifted Tessie's diary and keys, recovered and sheathed the sword, turned out the light and left the apartment. She proceeded directly to the bank and let herself into the basement with the key her husband left behind when he went overseas — he would have been careful to point out what that key was, and would likely have asked her to turn it in for him.

'Inside, she cleaned herself up with paper towels from the janitor's supply and then burned them in the furnace. And when the bank clock struck the first note of ten she went out, crossed behind the feed store to where Sheppard's car was waiting, opened the door with her right hand and shot him with his own pistol, which was held in her left hand.

'She did not even stop to close the door. She returned by the same route, entered the bank basement, crossed over and climbed the stairs and waited inside the door until Constable Westcott came along. When the constable and Frederick Thorne were at Ford Sheppard's car, she was calmly walking between the bank and post office. She entered Tessie Morgan's coupé, drove it to the lumber yard where she abandoned it, walked to the station and waited until midnight, at which time she called a taxi. When the driver finally arrived and informed her that Sheppard had been murdered, her alibi was complete.'

The commissioner scowled. 'Why was she trying to frame Thorne? He was part of her proof that Cotton Kendall was the scarecrow.'

'His work was done; he had convinced

the old man; he might prove to be a most embarrassing witness if he should want to visit his friend.'

The commissioner scratched his chin. 'And she went through all that to convince the old man, figuring that he would kick off pretty soon, which, by the way, I see he did.'

'That's it.'

'Then why didn't she just knock the old man off?'

Dickerson smiled. 'Because she had to produce a living Cotton Kendall before the old man died; it would have been too easy for Prudence Heath to claim the whole estate on the grounds that Kendall, even though listed as only missing, was actually dead when his father died.'

The commissioner sighed hard. 'I'll admit she'll have a rough time explaining away that phony shooting job she pulled with this Mrs. Tolbert for a witness, but you'll have just as rough a time proving that she returned to Sudwich at nine-five instead of midnight. They'll throw that at us in court at every turn.'

Dickerson smiled grimly. 'I'm rather

hoping they do, sir. That's where she made her biggest mistake. I have the affidavits of the towerman, bridge tender, the train's brakeman, fireman, engineer, two conductors and, thus far, eight passengers that the New York express which left South Station at ten o'clock on Thursday night, March twenty-first, did not stop in Sudwich. Apparently everyone in Sudwich, including Marion Kendall, was so excited about the murders that they failed to notice the fact.'

We do hope that you have enjoyed reading this large print book.

Did you know that all of our titles are available for purchase?

We publish a wide range of high quality large print books including:
Romances, Mysteries, Classics
General Fiction
Non Fiction and Westerns

Special interest titles available in large print are:
The Little Oxford Dictionary
Music Book, Song Book
Hymn Book, Service Book

Also available from us courtesy of Oxford University Press:
Young Readers' Dictionary
(large print edition)
Young Readers' Thesaurus
(large print edition)

For further information or a free brochure, please contact us at:
Ulverscroft Large Print Books Ltd.,
The Green, Bradgate Road, Anstey,
Leicester, LE7 7FU, England.
Tel: (00 44) **0116 236 4325**
Fax: (00 44) **0116 234 0205**

THE EMBANKMENT MURDER

Gerald Verner

A man's body is found on the Embankment missing a canine tooth, which turns up nearby on the ground. It is the first in a chain of grotesque murders that all involve the same M.O.; though on subsequent occasions, the tooth has been taken. Out of his depth, Detective Inspector Evens of Scotland Yard calls in London's foremost amateur criminologist, Professor Barrington. What is the connection between the murdered men — and can Barrington bring the criminal to justice before he himself is added to the tally of the dead?

THE BODY LOOKS FAMILIAR

Richard Wormser

While Chief Assistant D.A. Dave Corday
lurks in wait for Deputy Chief of Police
Jim Latson and his girlfriend in her
apartment, his cool plan for murder and
revenge is the only thing on his mind.
At gunpoint, Corday takes Latson's own
weapon and drills six bullets into the
woman: now all he has to do is let the
evidence point to the 'guilty' man. But
Latson's a dangerous foe to cross — and
when Captain Martin of Homicide takes
the case, the heat is on for them both . . .

THE LAST STEP

Tony Gleeson

The victim, found shot to death on a public stairway, is a recently paroled prison inmate. Is it a deliberate act of vengeance, and does it mean the killer will be looking for more victims? Detectives Jilly Garvey and Dan Lee are put on the case; but their colleague Leon Simpkins, who has taken an unexpected interest, seems to find it all striking uncomfortably close to home. Before they can solve the crime, the three will have to uncover deep secrets, with a profound effect on almost everyone involved.